THE CESSION

Contents

Dedication

This book is dedicated to my wife Kathleen, who tolerates me while I write it for reasons that escape me.

Acknowledgements

This book would not have been possible if it weren't for my mother's influence. She taught me never to take myself too seriously and respect everyone who deserves it. Of course, identifying the people who deserve respect is a challenge, but I work through it when possible.

She informed me every day that something would happen, and she has always been right. When things went wrong, she readily identified it as "bad shit," and when something went well, that was just to be expected.

She possessed the gift of simplifying complex things by stating, "Always start at the beginning." And in tough times, you could still find something to laugh about even when things went wrong.

I must also acknowledge my wife Kathleen, who spent countless hours reviewing the contents and encouraged me to write this book.

Enjoy The Cession!

CHAPTER ONE

The Beginning

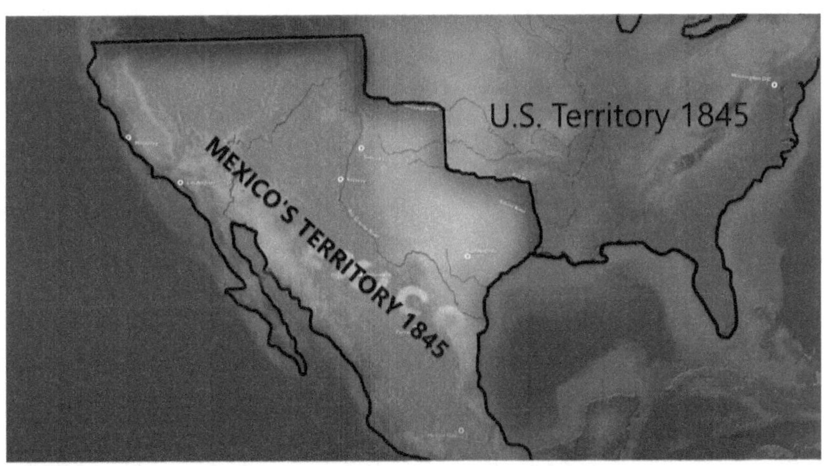

My mother always said that to understand the problem and achieve a correct outcome, you must first start from the beginning. The beginning lies in history, and like most, I wouldn't say I like history. But that is where we must go to understand what is happening in the United States today.

The beginning for me started with a lecture by Professor Martin Norris at the University at Albany in January of 2023. It began on a cold evening on a newly plowed State of New York Campus at the lecture Center. I was surprised how few were in attendance to hear Professor Norris. The Professor was renowned for honest, down-to-earth layouts of the world's history and, occasionally, a good conspiracy theory. Tonight, his topic was "The United States' interaction with the world and how it relates to the present." As I said, I was surprised how few were in attendance, but then again, no one wants to hear bad news.

Once seated in the Center, I waited patiently for Professor Norris to take the podium and begin speaking. I watched him stroll across the stage area of the hall and briefly stare into the gallery area of the building. The Professor started, "I can see the cold evening has limited the number of people here tonight. Of course, I suppose I could be the cause of the small turnout." Like most of the others in the room, I started to laugh. It was apparent the Professor had a sense of humor, and he was a seasoned speaker. I was surprised to hear his voice as it did not fit the body of the person standing on the stage. His voice was a higher pitch than one would expect from a plump, short man.

After a short pause, the Professor begins the lecture by saying, "To find the beginning, we must return to around eighteen forty-eight. Yes, that may sound unbelievable, but it all began in the United States around eighteen forty-eight. Looking back at the events over the last few years, one must wonder what we thought would happen with a border open to all who arrived to enter the United States. The warning signs were all flashing danger as our elected officials, the band in Washington, continued to play on like Nero as Rome burned." I took a moment to look around the room at the other attendees. At that early point in the lecture, I felt sure that the Democrats would be heading for the nearest door to escape. To my surprise, no one left their chair and fled from the hall, but I did notice two men sitting off to my left that appeared to be out of place at a history lecture. The men in perfectly tailored suits sat upright, almost as if in a uniform. I could not understand why they seemed out of place, but whatever the reason, I felt they should not be there at a history lecture on a college campus. But there they were, without expression on their faces, waiting for the Professor to continue.

I could tell from the first few sentences the Professor spoke that this was not a pep talk about how well things were going in the country. My head had barely turned back forward as the Professor continued. "By all appearances, the open border was more of a plan to process migrants quickly into the country with minimum security checking and the hopes and dreams that everything would be okay. Maybe the controlling political party, I will leave their name to you. They believe everyone allowed a free pass into the country would feel gratitude and vote for a single party as a thank you. Or maybe add population to several areas of the country they controlled to increase their congressional seat count. Perhaps it was a gesture to show people how great the United States is by allowing unfettered entry. As one Senator remarked, we were enabling unrestricted entry because we needed people to pick our vegetables and make babies to rebuild the population of the country. Still, others claimed the border was closed and people arriving were being returned to their country of origin. This claim, of course, for the most part, was strictly untrue. Remember The Wizard of Oz said, 'Ignore the man behind the curtain,' when Toto the dog pulled it back for all to see."

The Professor briefly looks down at his notes and then continues, "Whatever the reason, the President, that's right, our President, guided it all. He was lost in his little world and unable to see or understand the dangers his policies created. Whatever is going on, planned or unplanned, things are about to change forever, and the people who believe they are in charge are about to be awakened to a nightmare of their creation. The cost of utopia is about to be realized; the only question remains: who will pay the price for it."

The Professor paused and lifted a glass of water to his lips before he continued. "In summary, over three years of an open border have allowed millions of immigrants to enter the United States. Most are unchecked and un-verified, and their identity is often false or hidden. At the same time, Border Control Agents have indeed captured and deported many on the terror watch list, unfortu-nately, murderers, sex offenders, human traffickers, and other felons, thousands of whom have successfully made the journey dispersed into the country, never to be seen again.

It became so ridiculous one illegal migrant created Tik-Tok videos instructing others how to exercise squatter's rights into empty or for sale homes and have babies to game the welfare system for thousands of dollars.

Sanctuary cities continued to absorb the flow of im-migrants bussed, flown, or transported by other means until they occupied every square foot of space available and filled it with illegal immigrants. Non-sanctuary cities cried out for help and demanded a closing of the border, but the administration brushed aside their cries, claim-ing a hidden prejudice against immigrants. Finally, even sanctuary cities have started to sound the alarm about the unsustainable flow of immigrants into the country." The Professor paused again and lowered his head as if reviewing his notes.

The Professor raised his head and spoke softly, "Why is this happening? As the United States enters an era of inability to cover the cost of this uncontrolled flow of people from all corners of the world, the underlying plan,

I believe, is about to be executed. A plan that waited for over one hundred and seventy-five years for the right time to attack and weaken the United States from within. One hundred and seventy-five years of waiting for the right circumstances to avenge a war of our ancestors. They have patiently waited, and now, the time has come for them to recover what Mexico believed to be rightfully theirs."

I took a moment and sat back slowly in my chair. I was unsure if I was attending a lecture on history or a conspiracy theory seminar. The only thing I was sure of was that I would not leave this room until I heard the entire story from Professor Norris. Before the Professor could continue, I quickly looked around the large room. My imagination may have gotten the best of me, but I thought I saw the two men in those slick suits taking photos of the people attending the lecture. Now I am seeing things, I thought.

Professor Norris continues, "Very few United States citizens remember that at one time, several states in the lower western part of the United States were Mexican territory. Those included California, Arizona, Nevada, Utah, part of Colorado, part of New Mexico, a large part of Texas, a small part of Kansas, and a small part of Oklahoma. These states made up over half of Mexico's total landholding. Well, what happened to force Mexico to give up such valuable land?

The Mexican Cession, officially called the Treaty of Guadalupe Hidalgo, ended the Mexican-American War and was signed on February 2, 1848, at Guadalupe Hidalgo, a city to which the Mexican government had fled. The major concession from Mexico in the Cession was its exchange of fifty-five percent of its territory to the United States for fifteen million dollars. What a great deal, fifteen million dollars for all that land. As a result of the Treaty, including the official recognition of the State of Texas, the United States enlarged its territorial boundaries by more than sixty percent. It stretched its borders from sea to shining sea. In only four years, from its annexation and statehood of Texas in 1845 to the lands gained by the Mexican Cession in 1848, the United States had become a global power. The country also enjoyed its position as a nation bordered by a conquered foe to its south, a sparsely populated Canada to its north, and the Pacific and Atlantic oceans on its west and east coasts.

I am sure anyone can understand how Mexico felt about giving up all of the territory it believed it rightfully owned. Does anyone here tonight think they were pissed? The Mexican government's problem was that it was 'outgunned' by a two-to-one margin of men and weapons and unable to fight to defend the territory against the United States. The surrender to the United States left, at best, a bitter taste in Mexico's mouth, and the payment of fifteen million dollars did little to make the taste go away. The Cession in 1848 of all that territory has never sat well, and the Mexican people have long memories of what they believe they were cheated out of by the United States. The problem was that the United States was the 'bully on the block,' and Mexico was without any leverage to correct what they believed to be wrongdoing. Mexico has been biding its time for over a hundred and seventy-five years to gain leverage against the United States. The open border policy was the break they waited for; they are taking full advantage of it today.

Has anyone ever wondered why Mexico allows people worldwide to move freely from its southernmost border to its northern border unrestricted?" There was a brief pause, "Come on, raise your hands if it crossed your mind. Let's see those hands." The Professor waited, and almost everyone raised their hand, including me. "Okay," he restarted, "In the United States, we watch the caravans of people moving through Mexico on the news almost daily. It would be hard to believe the Mexican government did not know the caravans were traveling on foot through their country while they did nothing to stop or slow that migration. What is more concerning is that the migrants were not only from South American countries. Many countries worldwide allow citizens and criminals to be emptied from their prisons to pick up and move without legal documents for travel to the United States.

It gets worse; the open border was a prime opportunity for terrorist and criminal organizations to make their move and slide into the United States to build cells and work from within. An untold number of people from the Middle East have crossed the United States borders in a short period. Surveillance cameras along the border have videoed large groups of men dressed in camouflage and carrying weapons into the United States. These so-called gotaways number in the thousands or tens of thousands. Middle Eastern people who call the United States the big Satan are allowed to walk directly in and travel throughout the country without proper identification with intentions unknown. Anyone watching the evening news is well aware of Middle Easterners chanting 'death to the United States and Israel.' The hatred of the United States in these countries can not be understated."

The Professor took a moment and lifted his water glass again before continuing, "Mexico alone could not pressure the United States, with only the support of the Middle Easterners who had slipped into the country. They would need a great deal more to push forward their agenda. China became a willing participant to advance Mexico's lead. Has anyone asked how many Chinese citizens have reached the United States-Mexican border? Many Chinese military-age men walk into the United States with no questions asked. The Chinese, like the Mexicans, have long memories of wrongs done in the past to their countries and people. Mexico and China have had issues dealing with the United States and other Western countries. And like Mexico, China has a debt to settle with the United States and the West.

We know why Mexico is upset. We took their land, but why is China also upset? Well, let me take a little time to explain why China has a problem with the United States. A quick look back at history reveals In 1839, England went to war with China because it was upset that Chinese officials had shut down its drug trafficking racket and confiscated its dope. It is hard to believe the British were in the illegal drug business, but they were. Possibly the biggest snobs in the world were, at one time, drug dealers.

Stating the historical record so plainly is shocking to most, but it's true, and the consequences of that act are still felt today within China.

So what happened? The Qing Dynasty, founded by Manchurian clans in 1644, expanded China's borders to their farthest reach, conquering Tibet, Taiwan, and the Uighur Empire. However, the Qing turned inward and isolationist, refusing to accept Western ambassadors because they were unwilling to proclaim the Qing Dynasty as supreme above their heads of state.

Foreigners, even on trade ships , were prohibited from entry into Chinese territory. The exception to the rule was in Canton, the southeastern region centered on modern-day Guangdong Province, which adjoins Hong Kong and Macao. Foreigners were allowed to trade in the Thirteen Factories district in Guangzhou, with payments made exclusively in silver. Even back then, cash was king.

The British gave the East India Company a monopoly on trade with China, and soon, ships based in colonial India were vigorously exchanging silver for tea and porcelain. However, the British had a limited supply of silver and needed something else to use for trade.

Starting in the mid-1700s, the British began trading opium grown in India in exchange for silver from Chinese merchants. Opium , an addictive drug that illegal dealers can refine into heroin , was prohibited in England but was used in Chinese traditional medicine."

The Professor stopped a moment to clear his throat before continuing. "However, recreational use was illegal and not widespread. That changed as the British began shipping in tons, that's correct, tons, of the drug using a combination of commercial loopholes and outright smuggling to get around the ban. Chinese officials taking their cut abetted the practice. American ships carrying Turkish-grown opium joined in the narcotics bonanza in the early 1800s. Consumption of opium in China sky-rocketed, as did profits. The Chinese people were quickly becoming drug addicts by drugs supplied by the Western world. It sounds like what is happening in the United States today, right?

Well, the Daoguang Emperor became alarmed by the millions of drug addicts and the flow of silver leaving China. As is often the case, the actions of a stubborn idealist brought the conflict to a head. In 1839, the newly appointed Imperial Commissioner Lin Zexu instituted laws banning opium throughout China. He arrested seventeen hundred dealers and seized the crates of the drug already in Chinese harbors and even on ships at sea. He then had them all destroyed. That amounted to two and a half million pounds of opium thrown into the ocean. This event, I believe, is likely where the term 'flying fish' came from." Quipped the Professor as the hall echoed with a low-level laugh.

The Professor displayed a brief smile before speaking again. "Angry British traders got the government to promise compensation for the lost drugs, but the treasury couldn't afford it. The British decided war would resolve the debt with China, and the Chinese made the first shots when they objected to the British attacking one of their merchant ships. The Chinese were not a match for the British forces and needed to concede to end the war. Chinese authorities indicated they would allow trade to resume in non-opium goods. Lin Zexu even sent a letter to Queen Victoria pointing out that as England had a ban on the opium trade, they were justified in instituting one also. The letter was intercepted and never reached the

Queen, but it eventually appeared in print in the Sunday Times.

Instead, the Royal Navy established a blockade around Pearl Bay to protest the restriction of free trade in drugs. H. M. S. Volage's Captain, unwilling to tolerate the Chinese "intimidation," fired a broadside at the Chinese ships. H. M. S. Hyacinth joined in the fight, and one of the Chinese ships exploded, followed by three more Chinese vessels sunk.

Seven months later, a full-scale expeditionary force of forty-four British ships launched an invasion of Canton in the southern province of China. The British military had steamships, heavy cannons, Congreve rockets, and infantry with rifles capable of accurate long-range fire. Chinese troops , "bannermen," were still equipped with matchlocks accurate only up to 50 yards and a rate of fire of one round per minute.

The Royal Navy swiftly destroyed antiquated Chinese warships. British ships sailed up the Zhujiang and Yangtze rivers, occupying Shanghai along the way and seizing tax-collection barges, strangling the Qing government's finances. The Chinese armies suffered defeat after defeat as the British advanced.

When the Qing sued for peace in 1842, the British, being the victor, set their terms. The Treaty of Nanjing stipulated that Hong Kong would become a British territory and that China would establish five treaty ports where

British traders could trade anything with anybody they wanted. A later treaty forced the Chinese to recognize the British as equals and grant their traders formally favored status.

For the life of me," The Professor remarks, "Why should the Chinese be mad? Anyway, Imperialism was on the upswing by the mid-1800s. France also muscled into the treaty port business in 1843. The British soon wanted even more concessions from China, unrestricted trade at any port, embassies in Beijing, and an end to bans on selling opium in the Chinese mainland. Once again, this poisoning the Chinese people with drugs distributed by the Western world. Another tactic the British used to further their influence was registering the ships of Chinese traders they dealt with as British boats to increase their leverage on trade control.

When you think things could not get worse, the pretext for the Second Opium War is comical in its absurdity. In October 1856, Chinese authorities seized a former pirate ship, the Arrow, with a Chinese crew and an expired British registration. The captain told British authorities that the Chinese police had taken down the flag of a British ship. The British demanded the Chinese governor release the crew at once. When only nine of the fourteen returned, the British began a bombardment of the Chinese forts around Canton.

British Liberals, under William Gladstone, were upset at the rapid escalation and protested fighting a new war with China for the sake of the opium trade in parliament. However, they lost seats in an election to the Tories under Lord Palmerston. He secured the support needed to prosecute the war with China, and this unjust war continued." The Professor pauses again to allow attendees to absorb what he is presenting.

He continues, "China was not in a position to fight back. China was embroiled in the devastating Taiping Rebellion, a peasant uprising led by a failed civil service examinee claiming to be the brother of Jesus Christ. The rebels had nearly seized Beijing and still controlled much of China, weakening the Chinese government.

Once again, the Royal Navy demolished its Chinese opponents, sinking twenty-three junks in the opening engagement near Hong Kong and seizing Guangzhou. Over the next three years, British ships worked their way up the river, capturing several Chinese forts through naval bombardment and amphibious assault.

Not to be outdone in all of the craziness, France joined in the war. Its excuse was the execution of a French missionary who had defied the ban on foreigners in Guangxi province. Even the United States became briefly involved after a Chinese fort took potshots at a long distance on an American ship." Professor Norris stops momentarily before saying, "What, did you think the United States wasn't going to try and cash in on this mess? Are you kidding? In the Pearl River Forts Battle, a U.S. Navy force of three ships and two hundred eighty-seven sailors and marines took four forts by storm, capturing one hundred and seventy-six cannons and fighting off a counterattack of three thousand Chinese infantry. Still, the United States claimed to be officially neutral during all this.

Oh, and let us not forget Russia. Russia did not join in the fighting but used the war to pressure China into ceding a large chunk of its northeastern territory, including the present-day city of Vladivostok.

When foreign envoys drew up the subsequent Treaty in 1858, the terms were even more crushing to the Qing Dynasty's authority. The Treaty designated ten more cities as treaty ports, foreigners would have free access to the Yangtze River and the Chinese mainland, and Beijing would open embassies to England, France, and Russia.

The Xianfeng Emperor initially agreed to the Treaty but then changed his mind, sending Mongolian general Sengge Rinchen to man the Taku Forts on the waterway leading to Beijing. The Chinese repelled a British attempt to take the forts by sea in June 1859, sinking four British ships. A year later, an overland assault by eleven thousand British and six thousand seven hundred French troops took the forts.

When a British diplomatic mission came to insist on adherence to the Treaty, the Chinese took the envoy hostage and tortured many in the delegation to death. The British High Commissioner of Chinese Affairs, Lord Elgar, decided to assert dominance and sent the army into Beijing. British and French rifles gunned down ten thousand charging Mongolian cavalrymen at the Battle of Eight Mile Bridge, leaving Beijing defenseless. Emperor Xianfeng fled to safety. To wound the Emperor's "pride as well as his feeling," in the words of Lord Elgar, British and French troops looted and destroyed his historic Summer Palace.

The new revised Treaty imposed on China legalized both Christianity and opium and added Tianjin, the central city close to Beijing , to the list of treaty ports. It allowed British ships to transport Chinese indentured laborers to the United States and fined the Chinese government eight million silver dollars in indemnities. Let me repeat that: transport Chinese indentured laborers to the United States.

The Western presence in China became so ubiquitous and widely detested that an anti-Western popular revolt, the Boxer Rebellion, broke out in 1899. The hapless Qing Dynasty, under the stewardship of Dowager Empress Cixi, first tried to clamp down on the violence before throwing its support behind it just in time for a multi-national military force of U.S., Russian, German, Austrian, Italian, French, Japanese and British troops to arrive and put down the rebellion.

With all that said, the history between the Western world and China has been terrible at best. After understanding the history of China, the United States, and Europe, it is evident why China is moving forward with its world domination policies. The fentanyl being created in China and distributed around the world by Cartels and others is a payback for what was done to China over a hundred years ago."

Everyone in attendance sat motionless while the Professor detailed why China was unhappy with the United States and other countries worldwide. No one sitting there raised their hand to question the information the Professor was presenting, no one. The two men in slick suits were the only two I could see taking notes.

Professor Norris lifted a sheet of paper from the podium and continued, "How about today? Well, the Triads control organized crime in China. Due to their history of "patriotic" work supporting various political movements and factions, triads have allegedly been connected to the Chinese Communist Party (CCP), often via its related groups. Triad members are suspected to be members acting as agents of the party-state in achieving its political objectives of suppressing dissent, quelling protests, and silencing, intimidating, and coercing critics both at home and abroad, particularly in Hong Kong, Taiwan, and countries with high concentrations of ethnic Chinese. The CCP recognized the benefit of triads as part of their United

Front activities to neutralize opposition. The activities of the triads are supported by local government corruption and law enforcement authorities who ignore criminal behavior when influenced by the seniority of corrupt officials out of political convenience. Triads have become the principal money launderers for drug Cartels in Mexico, Italy, and elsewhere. They are reportedly money movers for the CCP elite and other government officials. The Triads give China the 'plausible denial' of involvement in the fentanyl trade in Mexico that is poisoning the United States and other countries around the world.

The open border has allowed the axis of evil to come together to create the perfect storm. Mexico, China, and the terrorists from the Middle East are infiltrating the United States to attack from within. Each Axis member has a different reason for participating, but all have targeted the United States. The Mexican Cartels are now in the position of a 'middleman' there to make a profit from all parties concerned.

We need to ask one question now that we understand a little of the bad blood history between the United States, Mexico, China, and the Middle East. What could go wrong with allowing an unfettered flow of migrants into the United States by way of the open border?"

The Professor stood silent for several moments, waiting for a hand to be raised by anyone sitting in the hall with a question or rebuttal comment. No one raised a hand or commented on what they had just heard. This lecture wasn't a conspiracy theory but a complete plan for someone to follow.

The Professor slowly continued, "Why would many people make such a dangerous trip from South America and other places worldwide? Why?" He repeated. "The United States has spent many years promoting itself as the most incredible place to live. All while allowing many of the countries of South America to slowly turn into failed states. The United States tries to play the hero and dump money into these countries as foreign aid. Frankly, most of the aid funds are siphoned away into the pockets of the corrupt politicians in those countries. The poor stay poor, and the wealthy politicians live high and flee to another country with all their money. I don't have a solid answer on controlling foreign aid, but handing over a check is not the way. Let me repeat: We have allowed a large group of failed states to be created in this hemisphere and are now paying the price for it."

After a pause, the Professor continued, "What about all the other countries dumping people into the United States? Please raise your hand if you know someone who fled to Russia or China for a better life in the past fifty years." He again paused before continuing, "Well, how about Haiti or Nigeria? Let me clarify that many migrating people are the sheep into which the 'bad guys' are being concealed by countries wanting to harm the United

States. Mexico wanted to recover all the territory lost in 1848 to the United States and now knows they have support from all over the world to achieve that goal. Let me repeat: Mexico wants all the land back from the United States."

The Professor picked up his papers and made one final comment before leaving the stage. "If you believe anything I have said here tonight is incorrect, please feel free to check it out yourselves, and if I have made an error, my e-mail address is on the brochure. I am always willing to listen to comments and corrections. I hope one of you contacts me and proves I am wrong about what will happen. Thank you for listening, and good night." And the Professor strolled off the stage into the shadows.

My evening ended with a long walk across the college campus to where I had parked my car. The cold air did little to dampen the information I had just heard from the Professor. Someone long ago stated that forgotten history is doomed to repeat itself. I was unsure if I got a history lesson or a vision of the future in the Professor's lecture. What was more concerning was that I was uneasy with either of them as I drove home. The history of China and the Western world could not have been any worse than it was. How many Chinese people must have died by the forced import of those drugs? And now China has turned the tables on the rest of the world, dumping the Fletanyl poison on the world.

My following thoughts were even more concerning. What if the Professor is correct and Mexico, China, and Middle Eastern terrorists are working together? The Cartels seem to be the only people happy with what is going on, and is it possible the United States has finally entered into a suicide pack to get our vegetables picked and make babies?

Chapter Two

The Calm Before the Storm

I spent the next two months thinking about what Professor Norris said in the January lecture in Albany. Is it possible that the Professor's conclusions were correct and that Mexico planned to recapture a large portion of the West Coast of the United States? After the lecture, I started watching the news and newspaper articles more closely, paying particular attention to who and from where the immigrants were coming. The headlines today read, 'Nine died while swimming the Rio Grande on Friday as deaths became commonplace this year after a migration shift pushed thousands to attempt the dangerous crossing. The Rio Grande has become a raging river of troubled waters separating Mexico and the United States.'

I'm not particularly eager to attach myself to conspiracy theories, and if something was going on, I wanted to see it for myself. I decided to spend my two-week vacation in Texas and travel to the southern border area. Three days later, I landed at Dallas Fort Worth airport to begin my fact-finding tour and hopefully discredit the good Professor.

I'm not too fond of airports, and I got lost while trying to locate the baggage claim area. Airports need one sign when you get off the airplane, 'Go this way to get your luggage' and nothing else. Instead, you find screens with an 'X' marking the spot where you are in the airport. No bread crumbs, no yellow brick road, nothing to guide you to the luggage claim area, only 'you are here' on a map marking the spot where you are lost.

As I turned away from the 'you are here' display, I noticed out of the corner of my right eye people who seemed familiar. I paused and stared for a moment. The two men from Professor Norris' lecture stood about thirty feet from me. I noticed they were still wearing identical, well-tailored suits, and their faces were still without expression. They looked just like the night they were in Professor Norris's lecture. Damn, I thought, this is a small world. Then, my mind began to race, and I was able to create my conspiracy theory. Maybe they were the men in black or the C.I.A. I had seen it in the movie plots just like this. Then, I laughed as I stood and watched the two men walk away, not noticing me or paying attention to what I was doing.

As I picked up my rental car, I reviewed my plans for the trip. Where should I start my investigation? Well, where else but on the United States side of the Rio Grande near Eagle Pass, Texas, also known as ground zero for illegal crossings. And that is where I will be on the following day.

It was around eleven in the morning when I arrived. As I looked out along the river's edge, I could see two small inflatable floats with printed aquatic animals in bright colors lying close to the river under the Eagle Pass port of entry, what remains after immigrants died a day before trying to cross the cursed river. A Border officer told me that a parent placed their children in the floats and jumped in a deceptively calm river, only to be drawn into the whirlpools between pillars holding up the international bridge.

Floats of a Drown Family

He continued, saying that the spinning waters would pull under all who tread too near and deny access to the promise of freedom of the United States, sitting a short distance across the river in a last cruel twist of fate. With the money taken from the unfortunate family in their pocket, the coyotes that brought them to the river's edge stood silently as the family was swept away, turned, and left to collect the next group of immigrants who would attempt to make the crossing. The coyotes' job was complete once they got the family to the river, and the family's loss mattered little to these profiteers. Others were waiting to be guided to the river to make the river crossing, and daylight was always at a premium.

I could see the tears in his eyes as he finished the tale. The recovery of the bodies of misfortunate immigrants has become an almost daily occurrence, and no one was paying the coyotes to recover the dead, drifting bodies of adults and their children. The Rio Grande is a river that, on the surface, appears to be very calm and welcoming, taking the unaware and their loved ones to their death. With that said, the Officer turned and left me standing alone, trying to understand the cruelty it must take to watch as a family dies and do nothing but walk away.

Looking back, I realized the purpose of the coyotes leading the families to the river was that of a "Judas Goat." A Judas goat is a trained goat used in animal herding, leading others to be slaughtered. The immigrants believed they paid the coyotes to guide them to a safe crossing area. What happened was the immigrants were taken to a place to divert the border agents, allowing the smuggling of drugs, weapons, and other undesirables to cross at another point of the border. The agents would allocate their resources to save the misled families, leaving large border sections unprotected. It took a long time before I understood the Mexican cartel's sole motivation is money and power to move their agenda forward. Mothers, fathers, and children are not part of the game plan, and not following the game plan means death to a coyote at the hands of the cartel.

I am sure not all people making the hazardous trip have ill intentions for the United States. Many are looking to make a better life for their family. They chose the illegal entry method into the country because they believed the administration invited them to come in and making entry legally took years.

They formed caravans and other large groups to make the journey north, but before entry into the United States, rest assured each migrant paid a cartel to allow them to leave Mexico. Like waves crashing onto the shore, the migrants continued to flow north, looking for the land of promise. With little or nothing to return to, anywhere seemed to be a better place than the country they fled. Desperate people flee from countries without hope for themselves and their families. They were putting their lives on the line for a better place to raise their families. I am also sure that mixed in with many good migrants were the others whose sole mission was to gain entry into the United States. It is undisputed that gang members, terrorists, and other felons were among the migrants. Some countries took advantage of the mass migration and emptied their prisons, sending the criminals on the journey north. What better way to reduce the cost of housing unwanted violent people than to send them to the United States?

Caravan of Illegal Migrants Crossing

I now understood what the Professor meant when he spoke of how, while countries took advantage of dumping their convicts in the United States, others used the unfettered flow of people to move in their operations undetected. Terrorists saw the open gates as a way to infiltrate the country to strike from within. The cartels saw the opportunity to 'set up shop' in a new market dealing in drugs and human trafficking. China saw the open door policy as a way to access the heart of the United States colleges and corporations. I remember reading it, and it is well known by most observers that the Chinese have, for many years, based their entire economy on theft. Why should they spend money on development when they can steal it and produce it for less? The open border gave China a rapid transit system into the heart of the United States, mostly unchecked.

According to the Professor, Mexico had planned on a much grander scale; they wanted back the land they had given up in 1848 to the United States. The plan was to flood the United States with illegals and slowly push out the U.S. population. And what a start, in just over three years, about fifteen million people crossed the border. That number equals almost half of the entire population of California in just three short years. Mexico must have smiled when liberals forced U.S. Schools to include Spanish-speaking teachers and other ethnic training—three short years with no end in sight.

Everyone involved had their own goals to achieve through the mass intake of migrants, and the United States was allowing it all to happen by way of poor leadership. Republicans blame the Democrats, and the Democrats blame the Republicans. The truth lies in the middle, but all parties are now at fault. Three years of the misguided open border policy have allowed millions of undocumented people to flow into the United States. I read in a magazine where scholars tried to figure out how many of these undocumented people were likely to be gang members, terrorists, felons, or whatever other designation of criminal. This venture yielded numbers of each unwanted type of person but not their names or addresses. To state there are ten thousand terrorists, unnamed, living somewhere is not very reassuring. Worst yet, estimating there are ten thousand gang members we have allowed to enter the country. The policy is that we will find them after you or your family are assaulted or killed by one of these gang members. That is, of course, unless a sanctuary city protects them, and we can not deport them or prosecute them.

The world is watching in total amazement as the total failure of the border unfolds. The United States is slowly being reduced to a third-world country before everyone's eyes.

I now understand why the southern states began busing and flying the illegals to other parts of the country. Sanctuary cities like New York and Chicago filled quickly to capacity, with the migrants housed in luxury hotels and provided free food and credit cards. The cities were now converting schools into housing and recreational facilities to overflow housing. Sanctuary states, like California, began to supply medical care along with all other assisted living funds. Why would the illegals not come to the land where everything is free?

If the Professor was correct, the stage was now set, and the actors of this drama watched and waited for the United States to collapse or self-destruct under the pressure that arrived on its shores. Millions of people with little or no means of support invaded the United States, draining the resources and expecting other citizens to pay for them. How long this could be allowed to continue before the point of no return was anyone's guess.

Back in my hotel room, Fox News reported that true to form, a congressperson created a bill to present to Congress requesting low-income housing be updated and built to meet the 'green agenda standards' and reduce emissions to zero. I believe this bill was intended to help relieve the housing shortage of the lower class, but rest assured, housing constructed under this bill would be used to house illegal immigrants.

Exhausted, I took out the travel guide to see things to do in Mexico. The town of Ciudad Juárez popped up several times in the brochures I was thumbing through. It seemed like a great next stop on my investigative vacation, and I decided Ciudad Juárez was the place I would see.

The following day, I found myself traveling to El Paso, Texas. I discovered in the book that Ciudad Juárez, Mexico, is a short trip across the Ysleta-Zaragoza International Bridge from El Paso, Texas, on the U.S.A./Mexico border. These two cities lie together surrounded by desert and mountains, separated only by the almost dried-up Rio Grand River. You can cross the border on foot; walking takes only a few minutes. Unbelievable, in minutes, a short foot walk over the international bridge from one city to another, from the U.S.A. to Mexico.

Walking is easy when crossing the border from El Paso to Ciudad Juárez. Leaving the U.S., you pay a few pesos at the gate and then walk across the bridge. It is as simple as that. Nobody questions you, and you don't need to show your passport or any other identification to enter

Mexico. On your return trip to the U.S., expect long lines and a passport and other papers will be required to make your return. Ironically, Juárez is considered one of the world's most dangerous cities. In contrast, El Paso, Texas, is consistently voted one of the safest cities in the U.S., and both are within walking distance.

My reading earlier in the day brought to my attention that in the years since 2010, the violence decreased in Juárez because the federal security forces occupying the city, who were , largely withdrew in 2011, and the Sinaloa Cartel eventually . But Ciudad Juárez's turnaround was temporary. As a result of the open United States border, increased competition between cartels, new armed factions, and local gangs, in only one year. Juárez, Mexico, is the perfect place for the Axis of Evil to meet. Juárez, Mexico, is where the Axis can see the enemy of the United States and be protected simultaneously.

My trip to disprove the Professor was failing, and It appears Professor Norris was right in his evaluation of the world. I traveled along the Texas-Mexican border for the rest of my vacation and visited the cities and towns inside Mexico, watching for any sign of the conspiracy, without success.

"The Constitution is not a suicide pact" comes to mind time and time again. The words express the belief that constitutional restrictions on governmental power must be balanced against the state's and its people's survival needs. An outsider would question the government's or the people's survival under the leadership that allowed the border to remain open to all who arrived without identifying who and what they were.

My two-week vacation ended with more questions than answers concerning the Professor's lecture. Like all conspiracy theories, I could not prove Mexico wanted the territory back or the Chinese were getting revenge for the poisoning of their people. Stating gang members and terrorists gaining access to the United States was obvious and, as far as an attack, just a matter of time.

If the Professor is correct, everything appears in place, and it is just a matter of time for the Axis of Evil to finalize their plans. As for me, I felt sure they all needed to meet in a single location like Juárez to put everything into motion. I was also sure there was no room for mistakes by anyone involved, as a misstep would result in a failed takeover. The end of the United States was not yet within reach, but the image of its collapse was on the horizon for anyone other than people who were blind.

CHAPTER THREE

The Interview

It was just over a month since I returned from my Mexico border vacation seeking the basis for Professor Norris's conspiracy theory. Professor Norris was convinced the illegal migration into the United States was a Mexican plan for the return of several U.S. States to Mexico. I would agree the flood of migrants into the United States was a severe problem, but to leap to a forced return of land to Mexico, I could not find a connection.

I witnessed firsthand the dangers people were willing to incur in their flight to a better life, but not an indication of a conspiracy to retake the land lost to the United States in 1848. If that was an underlying plan, it was well hidden from view by the average person.

A week later, on a Wednesday morning, my usual life course began to take an unforeseen detour. A knock at my front door forever changed my opinion of Professor Norris's theory. When I answered the door, the two men from the lecture and the airport in Dallas stood in their well-tailored suits and still without expression. My conspiracy theory from the Dallas airport was standing right before me, holding a federal badge in each of their hands. The taller man spoke, "Good morning, Mr. Thorn. I am special agent Moore, and this is special agent Goodhead from the Department of Homeland Security. May we come in and speak with you?" I slowly opened the door to allow them to enter my living room before speaking. "What can I do for you, gentlemen?" I started. The shorter of the two men spoke next. "We just have a few questions about your activities over the last, well, shall I say, a few years."

Baffled, I invited the two men to sit down, and I am sure my face showed the total disbelief of someone asking me questions of the last few years. I sat down and briefly thought to myself, what could be so interesting in my life to have Homeland Security agents at my home? This time, the taller of the two men started the conversation. "Mr. Thorn, have you had occasion to visit Mexico during the last year?" I sat back on the soft sofa, and an image of 'good cop, bad cop' came to mind. I replied, "Well, I spent a few weeks there earlier this year sightseeing. Is that what you are talking about?" "Pardon me, sir," the shorter man started. "We are not here to answer questions; we are here to ask them, and you are to answer them, understood, sir?" I raised my hands and replied, "Well, okay." I repeated my first answer, "I spent a few weeks there earlier this year." The shorter man said, "And what exactly did you do at the border, sir?" "I guess I just looked around at the river and took in the sites," I replied. The next question surprised me, "And what did that border patrol agent tell you what was going on?" Then I realized these agents were watching me while I was on vacation. The real question was, why was I being watched?

I leaned forward before replying, "What exactly are you driving at, and what does it matter who said what to me?" The taller man cut in, "Maybe we should start at the beginning, and maybe we can wrap this entire thing up today." "Okay," I started, "exactly where is the beginning and the beginning of what?" The taller agent took control of the questioning. "Our investigation shows that in March of 2016, you requested tickets to a Donald Trump rally in Albany, New York, at the Pepsi arena. Is that true?" I stared straight forward before answering, "Well, yes, I did." The agent continued, "And you attended this rally with one Thomas Brophie, is that correct?"

I nodded, "Yes, Tom and I went to the rally for President Trump." The shorter agent quickly said, "Mr. Trump wasn't president then, was he?" I looked at him and said, "No, that is why he was having a rally. If he were president, he would not have needed the rally, now would he." "And did you know at that time that Mr. Brophie worked for the Department of Justice?" the taller agent said. I replied, "Yes, I knew Tom worked for the Department of Justice, and I did not hold that against him. We went to the rally to see Mr. Trump in person and were impressed by how he presented himself. Does that answer your question concerning the rally of 2016?" The taller man continued. "And how much of the things Mr. Trump spoke about that evening did you believe?" The interview began to titter on the bizarre at this point. "Well," I started. "I don't take something someone tells me as real until I check it out and find the facts to support their claims. I listen, evaluate, and decide whether it is true. As far as Tom goes, you must ask him what he believed from the rally, as I can not comment on his thoughts."

The agents made a slight pause before asking the next question. This time, the shorter agent began the questions. "Let us move closer to today. Did you attend a lecture by Professor Norris earlier this year?" I replied, "Yes, I did." "And were any of your friends or associates in attendance for this lecture?" He followed up. I turned my head to the left before speaking, "I don't believe I saw anyone I knew at the lecture." The taller agent asked, "And what did you think about the Professor's ideas he expressed in the lecture?" My reply was terse, "Interesting conspiracy theory."

The agent continued, "Well, you did travel to the border and ask many questions, did you not?" "You know I was in Texas and Mexico because I saw you two at the Dallas airport. I was taking in the sights and enjoying my vacation, nothing more or nothing less." I answered. The short agent chirped in, "We know you were speaking with a border patrol agent about what was happening at the El Pasco crossing, and you asked many questions about the border. We know you made several crossings into Mexico over the two weeks. We know you were looking for something, and we would be grateful if you could tell us what you learned about during your little field trips into Mexico."

This interview lasted for over an hour, and the questions were, at best, out of line. They had asked personal questions about my friends, their finances, and their political views. I slowly stood up before answering the last question. "This is the answer to all of your questions. I went to a lecture and heard a conspiracy theory from Professor Norris. I took a vacation in Texas and traveled along the border to see what was happening if anything.

I took several day trips to Mexico to see the sights and enjoy Mexican food. I came home and could not prove or disprove what the Professor lectured about that night. And you two showed up at my home after following me across the country and watching what I was doing for two weeks in Texas. If anything, you are coming here today supports Professor Norris's conspiracy theory, at least in my mind. And before you ask, I was not in Washington, D.C., on January 6th. I thank you for coming. Please leave." I finished my closing statement, and they stood and walked out the front door, hopefully never to be seen again.

After the two agents left my home, they convinced me that Professor Norris might have the entire theory right. I had no way to prove it, but something big was going on with the border. It's much bigger than Donald Trump running for president or what happened on January 6th. The remaining question was what was happening and how long it would take to reveal the entire thing.

CHAPTER FOUR

The Final Plans

It was now evident that Homeland Security was aware of 'bad actors' planning something big in Mexico. Whether or not Homeland Security or other law enforcement agencies had solid evidence of what was intended or by whom was unknown. Whatever it was, it had to be significant in scope, involving several different entities. I kept thinking back to the lecture of Professor Norris; Mexico wanted all the territory they gave up during the

Cession of 1848 and would use the help of China, Middle Eastern terrorists, and immigrants to get it.

As for me, I had reached a dead end in my private investigation and needed to move on with my life. I can't put into words my feelings of uneasiness knowing the same people who allowed the border to remain open to all were the same people in charge of protecting the United States from a clear and present danger. Powerless is the only term I could come up with to describe how I felt. Powerless with nowhere to turn, with a story no one would believe about a threat of unknown origin from unknown people lurking in the shadows. But that is where I stood, at the mercy of incompetent, incapable people facing a threat to our existence.

Fifty-two degrees on an early Monday morning, three kilometers outside Ciudad Juárez, Mexico, was designated the Axis meeting place. The Mexican Government selected a single-standing home built on a hillside for its isolation and ease of securing the surrounding area. Trim trees and other natural vegetation surrounded the structure, yielding a clear line of sight to observe anyone or anything approaching. This house is in a perfect location, away from prying eyes and without the uncontrolled movement of unwanted traffic or people. A clear blue sky and a soft breeze accented the home when viewed from the single road leading in. The selected location is the essence of privacy, and the events of the next several hours would require absolute privacy.

Place of Meeting - Isolated House In Mexico

This morning was to be anything but typical as armored trucks, each bearing the Mexican Military markings, encircled the house in preparation for the main event. Mexican military personnel took their designated positions all around the building and set up their automatic weapons. In a clear display of force, the house looked more like a fort than a home this early Monday morning.

Just over an hour later, more military-looking vehicles started to arrive. These vehicles were unmarked, painted in camouflage, and some appeared to be in a state of disrepair. These vehicles belonged to the Cartels from different parts of Mexico. And just like the Mexican army, the Cartel personnel took positions alongside the Mexican military, forming an impenetrable ring of security around the single building.

Looking south, you could see dust along the single road obscuring the long caravan of official-looking limousines and armored vehicles as they approached. This house seemed to be a strange place to hold a meeting of such importance in a deserted area of no man's land with only Cactus plants to bear witness to the unfolding events.

A short time later, the caravan arrived, and the passengers began to depart the vehicles and walk a short path to the house. To an onlooker's surprise, the people exiting the transports were not all of Mexican descent. The convoy included many people from the Middle East, China, Afghanistan, Iran, several South American countries, and Mexico. Bodyguards and a translator accompanied the many special guests attending this event to ensure no misunderstandings at this critical meeting. Secrecy, security, and clarity were the message of the day. Today was the day to put into motion the final plans to overrun the United States and, according to many, kill the 'Great Satan.' As each guest passed through the large main door, a Mexican Army officer collected cell phones and all other recording equipment and placed them into a box with the guest's name attached. The only thing not collected by the Officer was the side arms that many of the guests carried.

Inside the house, you could hear the generator in the distance that supplied electrical power to the building. The center of the building was open and reconfigured to accommodate the large number of attendees. The walls of the large main room were all covered with wood paneling and white trim. A sign above a single door in several languages reads 'Restrooms,' directing guests to the building's facilities. Chairs were grouped and placed around a single large table, with additional chairs placed in rows behind each. The builder even added lighting to the ceiling and around the room's perimeter, removing all shadows. Four large fans were mounted on the ceiling and turned slowly to back up the air conditioning should it be needed. The windows were covered with a reflective film to block from view the inside of the room from the outside, creating a one-way mirror effect from within the room.

It was easy to see that this meeting was in the planning stages for an extended period. The details included several chefs waiting for the guests' dining requests in a separate kitchen and seating area. The builder of this place ensured there would be no reason to leave until the attendees completed all of their business.

Once inside the large main room, the specter of the mistrust was evident to all. Two heavily armed security men stood in the room's four corners. Each of the armed men represented a different group of people who would be attending the meeting. The Axis of Evil had agreed to work together, but it was clear they were not friends, and trust was not on the menu today.

Each guest walked single file into the main room, and a woman greeted them and directed them to where they would be sitting at the single large table. As each prominent guest sat, their translators and other support people took a chair behind them and slowly filled the room. In front of each prominent guest was a folder full of documents, and the wait staff placed a large pitcher of water with glasses alongside the folder. Other staff handed water bottles to all other attendees. Missing from the area was any microphone or amplified speaker system. All words spoken today were to be heard only by the attendees, and people outside the room could not listen to what was said.

The attendees for today's meeting included the heads of four of Mexico's Cartels. They are the Sinaloa Cartel, controlling much of the northwest; the Jalisco New Generation (CJNG) controls the west, mainly the Tierra Caliente region; the Gulf Cartel controls the north-east, centered around the border state of Tamaulipas, and the Los Zetas Cartel also controls portions of the north-east. Also in attendance was The President of Mexico, the Ambassador of China, the head of China's Triads, the Ambassador of Venezuela, the Ambassador of Argentina, the Ambassador of Ecuador, the Ambassador of Colombia, the Ambassador of Guatemala, two gang members from Haiti, two heads of Isis-K, two heads of Hamas, and the Revolutionary Guard Chief from Iran. Missing from the meeting was the Al-Qaeda leader, who refused to sit in the same room as Isis-K but who offered to be involved in any attacks on the United States during the operational activities.

With all finally seated, the meeting started just after ten A.M. with El Mencho, the alias of Nemesio Oseguera Cervantes, sitting at the head of the long table. The President of Mexico, although in attendance, decided to let El Mencho take the head position at the meeting. This arrangement gave the Mexican President a plausible denial that he conducted no such meeting should the need arise. El Mencho also arranged the security for the meeting, and others felt he should be at the head of the table. It is also well known that El Mencho could not take any chances because the U.S. Justice Department offered up to ten million dollars for leads that could result in his capture. And even with the U.S. Justice Department offering ten million dollars, no one was willing to take the U.S. Justice Department up on the offer. The attempts to capture El Mencho had turned into a vengeful game of chess, resulting in an endless succession of attacks and counter-attacks between the Mexican and U.S. governments and the head of the Jalisco New Generation Cartel, El Mencho. El Mencho had every reason to ensure a secure location and the proper security for the meeting, and with all that at stake, he was the perfect person to be at the head of the table.

El Mencho stood up and began the meeting with a warm greeting, nodding his head to each attendee as he looked around the table. El Mencho did not speak the name of any attendees for fear of mispronouncing a name and insulting someone sitting at the table. As he opened the meeting and began to talk, the translators were busy repeating his words as he went. "I don't need to thank any of you for coming here today, as we all have a score to settle with the United States. We here present today are under the understanding that you have been granted the authority to make decisions binding by the people or group you represent. If that is false, please raise your hand now, and you can leave this meeting." El Mencho paused and looked around the room for someone to raise a hand. He continued, "I do not see any hands raised, so instead of wasting valuable time, I will move directly to where we are with the original plan. I will lay out and detail the progress the Cartels have achieved, as that will give us the control we need to fulfill each of your objectives. The Cartels are going to continue to act as distributors of Fentanyl and other drugs within the United States and monitor their government responses to all of our activities in the upcoming months. We will not have direct involvement in any terrorist attacks as that would expose our operational houses. None of the missions would be possible without the intelligence we can supply. We will be like their C.I.A. and work from behind the scenes to gather and distribute critical information.

Let me bring all of us up to date on how far we have infiltrated the United States. We have established over two hundred monitoring and control centers in all but six states. We keep track of all immigrants' locations and activities from these control centers. We can control their gang activities and other criminal enterprises to disrupt the Gringo's law enforcement. We maintain control over the immigrants and the money they get from whatever source is returned to us by them. Hard to believe the Gringo's give the immigrants money, they send it to us, and we promote crime in the United States with the funds they supply.

We have overloaded several major U.S. cities with immigrants, forcing them to feed and house them. This overloading of their cities has severely drained their resources, and the U.S. funds are quickly running out. At last count, we have managed to move over fifteen thousand convicts released from South American prisons into the United States. The dumb Americans call them 'gotaways,' we call them soldiers. Moving in these soldiers means we have already been able to move a small army of disrupters into the United States. In the folder before you is a photo of a control center located in New Mexico that monitors immigrants and our other interests. Each of the centers is identical in that it allows any of our people to operate in any of the centers without additional training. We can direct and monitor your operations from each center in real time."

Each attendee opened the folder and inspected the photo before El Mencho continued. "And now, with the assistance of our friends, the Chinese hackers, we soon will be able to link into the U.S. power grids, many of the satellites providing G.P.S., and even the cell phone systems across the country."

One of Many Cartel Control Rooms

The Chinese representative stood, raised his hand, and spoke through his interpreter. "I would like to add that my hackers have identified a weakness in the U.S. cargo shipping routing system. G.P.S. automatically guides the large container ships in and out of the major ports to avoid collision with the bridges and shallow water. We discovered that if we disrupt the power on a bridge or other structure for a few seconds as the ship approaches, it can not precisely identify the course it needs to take to avoid a collision. We believe we could destroy U.S. infrastructure using this method for years." El Mencho waits for the representative to sit down before speaking. "As you can see, our efforts are already bearing fruit. The ability to take out shipping in the United States without firing a single shot. We sit in our control room and take over the United States from an armchair."

The President of Mexico stood and spoke next. "Mexico does not care about ships or cargo. We want the U.S. to return the territory they stole from us in The Cession of 1848. We need the immigrants moved into positions where the United States can no longer afford to support them. We need the immigrants to force the Americans out of our territory and replace them with our people. Drugs and other criminal activity are only sideshows re-quired to meet our goals. We are relying on our good friends from the Middle East to put pressure on the U .S. by attacking them in the South East and North East, forcing a withdrawal in our lost territories. We will also need guarantees that our good friends from the Middle East will not turn and attack us once we have completed our goals." The President of Mexico sat back down and waited for a reply.

The Revolutionary Guard Chief slowly rose from his chair before speaking in perfect English. "The Government and people of Iran have no issues with South American or the Mexican peoples. We are working toward the destruction of Israel and the Jews. After that, we will take our rightful place as leaders of the Islamic people and not create issues with countries or religions of the Americas." He then slowly sat down in his chair. The Ambassadors of the South American countries present were glad to hear Iran's response, but their faces showed they did not believe a single word of what he had said.

For a brief moment, there was silence in the room. One of the gang members of Haiti broke the peace by demanding to be heard as he stood up. "I am Jimmy Chérizier, the current leader of Haiti. I am here today with Renel Destina, the head of the Grand Ravine. We, the people of Haiti, have been victimized by the United States and some of the countries seated here for many years. Before we help with anything, we want to know how you will make this up to Haiti. I propose that all seated here today commit to payments to the people of Haiti. Five hundred million dollars would be a good starting point for us to agree on." He stood for a moment as the other attendees stared forward without speaking. Finally, El Mencho said, "We are not here today to work out payments for anyone. We are here to finalize operational plans to move our agendas forward. After we have succeeded, we can discuss other issues, such as payments, at another meeting."

One Isis-K attendee stood to deliver his message to the group, speaking through an interpreter. "I believe I speak for all Isis-K, Hamas, and all other true believer Islamic peoples. Christian people have been and continue to be at war with Islamic people. I can not sit here and guarantee any long-term peace with non-believers. We first should eliminate the 'Great Satan,' and then we should see what remains between us to be worked out." He then sat down.

Saying this alliance was on shaky grounds would have been a tremendous understatement. So many had come together, each with a different reason for destroying the United States. El Mencho proposed an hour break for those in attendance to discuss things amongst themselves before the meeting reconvened in the afternoon and let things settle down.

An hour later, the meeting reconvened. "I can see there will be no total agreement between us." El Mencho spoke the first words of the afternoon. El Mencho continued, "Maybe we need to look deeper into why we are here today. The Cartels and Mexico do not always get along, but sometimes, we must work together against a familiar foe. Working together gives balance, and Mexico exists in a state of balance. The Chinese Government and China's Triads do not always have the same goals, but they need each other to maintain control of China. Neither of them can retain control of the population of China without the other. I listen here today concerning how Islam will not allow Christians to exist. If you step back, you can see that stance is an out-of-balance view and will lead to your destruction. With that stance, you will achieve nothing. Today, I ask my Islamic friends to make a decision: accept balance or leave here with nothing. You must choose. We, Mexico, have waited over one hundred and seventy-five years for this time to regain our stolen lands, and we do not wish to waste this opportunity because some of us can not accept balance. I am now calling for another one-hour break so that you can discuss your position and purpose within the group again. Please enjoy some of our good food; hopefully, you can understand and find balance in your lives so we may continue this meeting."

El Mencho extended the one-hour break by half to allow everyone time to decide what part they would play in taking down the United States. The atmosphere was very uneasy as the attendees sorted out their differences. El Mencho was unsure if the Islamic attendees could find balance in their thinking and allow the meeting to continue. Suppose Isis-K and Hamas can not bring themselves to allow the existence of someone outside of their religion. In that case, it will be necessary for Isis-K and Hamas to be removed from all operations and sent home with nothing.

The meeting finally resumed about one hour and forty-five minutes after the break. One of the Hamas attendees addressed the meeting by way of an interpreter. "We have looked deep within us to find the things you have claimed caused balance. As you say, I stand here and can not find balance, but I can find necessity. We need to destroy Israel and to do so, we need to destroy the United States. We have concluded that our necessity is equal to your balance, and we agree not to wage a religious war on our friends who are helping us destroy Israel." With that stated, the Axis' of evil overcame the first hurdle of the day.

El Mencho accepted Hamas's response and began to move the meeting forward by addressing the President of Mexico. The Mexican President stood before speaking. "Next week, I will start to publicly pressure the United States into sending large amounts of money to the South American countries, claiming it will slow down the flow of immigrants. This public pressure will have several effects on our mission. First of all, it will cause turmoil within the population of the United States as people debate whether or not to send the money. Second, their U.S. politicians will be overwhelmed with answering the people they represent concerning the demand for money. Third, if they should agree and be dumb enough to send the money to us, we will take it and move the illegals in by way of the gotaways at night to continue overloading their system. I will continue to resist all calls for Mexican military on the border, and, of course, as always, I do not see any Cartel actions along the border." With that said, the Mexican President sat down.

El Mencho stood and looked directly down the long table toward the Iranian Chief and other terrorists seated at the table before speaking. "You must understand that we, the Cartels, are the eyes and ears of this complete operation. We have the control centers in place and are watching everything happening in the United States. The mission to take down the United States will not be successful by your people carrying out single hit-and-run attacks. It must be coordinated through us to place maximum pressure on the U.S. Our goal, Mexico's goal, is to force the United States to return the lands they stole from us. That will not be possible with a lot of small attacks. We will need an agreement to that right now to move forward." The Islamic attendees nodded in agreement, and the meeting continued.

El Mencho then turned toward the South American attendees before speaking. "You need to stay in contact with the families of those who made their way to the United States. We will be able to control the migrant's movements through their families. We can overload different parts of the U.S. as the need arises by moving large numbers of people into the most sensitive areas. As for the gang members from each of your countries, we have logged each of them and have their present locations in the U.S. We are using them for intelligence and moving our drugs. Our only issue with some of them is that they continue violating minor laws and getting arrested, drawing attention to our activities. Luckily, most stay in sanctuary cities and are released from jail quickly, limiting our exposure. I advise you not to contact the people you released from your sanitariums, as that, as the Gringo's would say, would be crazy." As El Mencho finished, a low laugh filled the room.

As the room became quiet again, El Mencho continued, "That leaves us with our good friends, the Chinese, and the Chinese Triads. We, the Cartels, depend heavily on the Fentanyl and other drugs supplied by China. I believe this has been an excellent means of generating money for both of us, and as for killing off Americans, they are collateral damage to us, but to you, they are revenge for the past. I am also very impressed as to how you tell the United States you are doing everything possible to curb the drugs leaving China while at the same time increasing the amount of drugs you sell to us. Very impressive." El Mencho stopped, lifted a glass of water, and slowly took a drink. As he returned the glass to the table, he again began to speak, "I will now return to something mentioned at the beginning of this meeting. China has connected the Cartels to their hacker's network. We will soon have access to and control many of the United States utilities and other infrastructures. Our control centers are currently being updated with the software to execute such a plan as we speak today, and the hackers have already been moved into the United States, awaiting orders to travel to the centers and execute the plan. I thank the Chinese for their assistance in this area." El Mencho again lifted the glass of water from the table and drank.

"And Now," El Mencho began, "I must address what could go wrong with this grand plan. We must keep the people we have moved into the United States under control to avoid key people from being arrested and deported at critical moments. If one of them gets arrested and faces deportation, they may leak some information to the U.S. Government. I realize they do not have the entire plan, but their Government could put pieces of information together and cripple us. We have a whole field full of buried gang members in Mexico, of people who could not keep their mouths shut. If we lose a large group of our key people in the United States, the acts of terrorism will only make the U.S. people mad, and our plans will be doomed."

El Mencho sat down, and the President of Mexico stood and addressed the meeting. "We all have much to gain by addressing our grievances with the United States. We have waited over a hundred and seventy-five years to regain what is rightfully ours. Each of you at this table has suffered in different but important ways at the hands of the United States. May each of our Gods guide us to victory, and for now, I say farewell to my good friends." And with that final comment, the meeting ended.

It was after seven P.M., and the air outside had already begun to cool as the sunset. Each attendee exited through the large building door and climbed into their awaiting vehicle. One by one, the convoy of vehicles headed down the single road leading south and away from where they had just planned the destruction of the United States. After all the attendees had left, the Cartel security and Mexican military followed, leaving only the support staff of the building. The staff disappeared into the night and returned from wherever they had come, never speaking about where they had been.

The desert sand around the building drifted as the wind blew, and the Cactus plants remained silent, hiding in the shadows. The building, now empty, was without sound, and the walls were what remained of all the witnesses to the events of that day. A house where the Axis of Evil had taken refuge to lay out its diabolical plan to destroy the United States was as empty as the foundation for the plan itself.

CHAPTER FIVE

Finally Enough

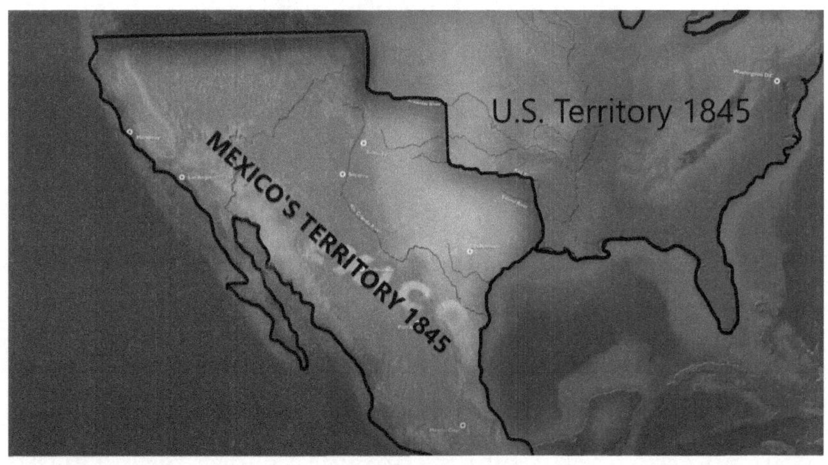

The Democrat Party stood silent as the illegal immigrants poured into the United States, and the Republicans fared little better. Maybe they believed the immigrants would be grateful and vote them continuously into office. Perhaps they were naive because they thought the people entering the country would change their ways and become good citizens. Whatever the reason, millions of people from all over the world streamed into the United States without any background on who these people were. Some wanted a better way of life, and others wanted to take advantage of an opportunity to gain access to the land of sheep. Still, others came to the United States to kill and take down the entire country. When the 'newcomers' arrived, no check box marked 'I am a good person' appeared on the entry form. No check box marked 'I will not rob or steal.' And no check box marked 'I am not a terrorist.' Simply stating I was fleeing prosecution in my home country was enough to gain entry into the land of plenty, only to be released with an appearance date far into the future.

The actual number of United States citizens lost to crime and accidents by illegals may never be known. The nightly news reports detailed the tragic events caused by illegals on our roads, along with the violent assaults and murders. It seemed that as long as the lower and middle-class societies were the only ones affected, nothing would change. It was only a matter of time before the people financing the elected officials and the officials themselves felt pain and suffering. It was a matter of time before their private security failed to protect them. It was a matter of time, and the clock was running.

One of the first to feel the pain was John & Marie Simmons. Their foundation was a substantial contributor to the Democrat Party. The foundation donated over twenty-one million dollars to the party and stood ready to donate more if needed. It is unclear whether they believed or not that many immigrants coming across the border were a problem, but they were determined to support the party. Their checkbook was in hand until their son at college disappeared, and a note arrived from an MS-13 gang demanding money for his life. The Simmons paid the money in vain, and they lost their son to the violence of the gang. When captured, the three men from El Salvador held up a middle finger to the press cameras. The men had been deported several times each and were only allowed to remain here by the latest administration of a sanctuary city. Besides, they were in New York City and felt confident that prosecution would be light in a sanctuary city, even for murder.

The beginning of the end occurred when Democrat Congressman Harris's daughter was murdered while on a morning jog in a park while attending college. Again, an immigrant who was arrested several times in New York City was released and relocated to Georgia. The man, an illegal immigrant, was arrested and charged with the brutal murder of this twenty-two-year-old girl and showed little if any remorse. He made his first court appearance smiling and planned to be released back to the streets in Georgia. He displayed a look of surprise when the court ordered him to be held without bail, facing a possible death penalty. "I demand to be deported!" The immigrant yelled as officers led him in chains from the courtroom to face his judgment day.

The violence plaguing the United States was finally taking a toll on the elite class, who felt isolated from the craziness. It was becoming apparent that even private security could not always protect you. With the large number of undocumented people wandering the United States, it was just a matter of time before someone close to you fell prey. The murder of Congressman Harris's daughter set into motion a personal vendetta to rid the country of thugs like the one who killed his daughter, and the Congressman was known for holding a grudge.

Congressman Harris knew that Congressional help was not in the foreseeable future as the two parties in power tried to use the crisis as a bargaining chip. The current President took almost three years to admit there was even a crisis at the border and accused the previous President of causing it. The current Secretary of the Department of Homeland Security found no issues with the border and declared the 'border is closed' after a visit. The Vice President, assigned to care for the border, remained locked away for fear of what she might say. The Vice President had a reputation for misspeaking and opening political rabbit holes. She was possibly the last person who should address issues about the border, and the administration kept her in the background as much as possible for that reason.

Congressman Harris watched as Americans suffered and died, but this time, the pain hit close to home with the murder of his only daughter. While others in Washington went through the motions under their circus tent, and as they say, 'the band played on,' Congressman Harris was working on a plan to revenge the death of his daughter.

Others attempted to stop the craziness at the border using all means possible. The Governor of Texas stepped forward and called up the state's National Guard to help secure the border. Cargo containers and razor wire began to line the border between Mexico and Texas. The Federal Government immediately filed suit to have all the barriers removed, and the battle between security and principal began. Texas made clear they had the right to protect Texas citizens while the Federal Government claimed they had sole control of the border and immigration. With the battle raging in the courtrooms of the United States, the immigrants began to storm the border, demanding entry as their right. Violence became the day's story as dedicated Guardsmen tried to hold the rushing immigrants back using their bare hands. Superiors ordered the border patrol officers to stand down and not assist, leaving the Guardsmen to fend for themselves.

Across the Gulf of Mexico, the State of Florida began passing legislation that gave every citizen of the State of Florida the right to carry a firearm. States around the country criticized the State of Florida, touting how it was ridiculous for everyone to have access to handguns. As I look back at the law passed in Florida concerning the right to carry a gun, I suppose the crazy part of carrying a handgun depends on which side of the assault you are on.

While Republican-led states tried to enact stricter laws about undocumented immigrants, New York State stood firm on its sanctuary grounds. All immigrants were welcome until the sheer number of bodies overwhelmed the cities. Hotels in New York City were filled with 'newcomers,' as were the schools and all other public facilities around the city. Reaching capacity, New York City began shipping the 'newcomers' to upstate New York Cities. The faster they shipped the 'newcomers' out of New York City, the quicker they arrived. The Mayor of New York City pleaded for assistance, but the Federal Government ignored his pleas. For now, at least New York State was on its own to care for the 'newcomers.'

Five million, ten million, fifteen million, or more undocumented people crossed into the United States to be lost and untrackable. Many are people searching for a better life, but unfortunately, many are here to prey upon the weakest of U.S. citizens. It is unclear how many of these undocumented people have been deported repeatedly over the years, but the number must be enormous.

Examples from all over the United States poured in as assaults, robberies, murders, and other crimes soared.

Undocumented people are sometimes arrested twenty or more times and released over and over without bail, only to disappear until another subsequent arrest. Motor vehicle deaths caused by immigrants, many of whom did not have a license, were reported far too often over a short period. So many families have perished at the hands of these undocumented immigrants driving without a license, drunk, or speeding with little or no regard for U.S. laws.

The violence continued across the country, and the country was on the verge of vigilantes roaming the streets of our cities. Our government protected the undocumented 'newcomers' while prosecuting legal citizens for defending themselves. If anyone addressed the illegals as a problem, support groups would label them racist or worse to stop anyone from questioning what was happening.

It was only a matter of time before someone would take the lead in overcoming the problem, and that time was approaching fast.

CHAPTER SIX

Creating Sanctuary

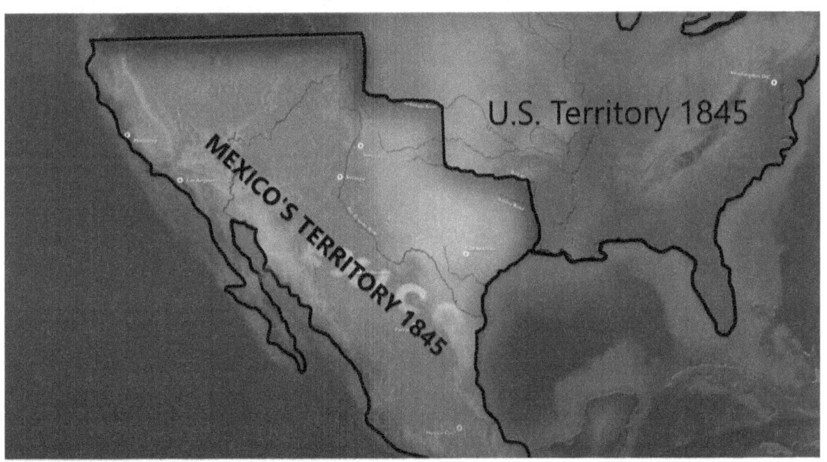

The crime wave across the United States became intolerable. The gangs controlled many major cities and were expanding to overwhelm law enforcement at an alarming rate. Cartels set up shops throughout the country, and the countries where the criminals migrated from refused to repatriate them. The crazy open border policy had come home to roost, leaving many afraid to leave their homes. The world watched as uncontrolled immigration was reducing the United States into a third-world country. The affluent hired private security, and everyone without the means to afford the luxury of private security began to stockpile weapons in their homes. The United States teetered on the brink of total civil unrest, a war between the haves and the have-nots.

The government officials elected to protect the people watched the rapid decay of the cities and attempted to dampen the damage they had done by referring to crime as growing pains. It seemed our politicians were deaf and blind or did not care. Finally, a group of seven congressmen created a new underground committee to address the problem and, if needed, step outside the system and take whatever necessary actions, approved or not. They needed a plan 'B'. A plan to remove undesirable immigrant criminals from the country. A drastic plan that no one had ever conceived or even dreamed of. The problem they faced was the Constitution, which laid out all the protections for people within the borders of the United States, whether illegal or not. They knew that whatever plan they decided to go with, the committee needed to sidestep the framework of the Constitution to make it work, and they were determined to make it work. Taking a quote from naval history, the committee adopted the phrase, "Damn the torpedoes, full speed ahead!"

Congressman Harris, whose daughter was murdered by an illegal immigrant, defined the scope of the operation in a secret memo for the other committee members as follows.

The Plan 'B' Outlined

First, the project will be funded through a 'Black ops.' Mr. Harris continued to define 'Black Ops' as a black operation or a covert or clandestine operation by a government agency, a military unit, or a paramilitary organization; it can include activities by private companies or groups. Key features of a black operation are that it is secret and not attributable to the organization carrying it out. The main difference between a black operation and one that is merely secret is that it involves a significant degree of deception, concealing who is behind it or making it appear that some other entity is responsible. As stated, our committee does not exist, giving us a plausible denial of any involvement should Plan 'B' be exposed.

Second, we have selected a location for this 'sanctuary island' off the coast of California. The selected island is located sixty-one miles off the coast of California. San Nicolas Island belongs to the U.S. Navy and is part of the Naval Air Center's Sea Test Range associated with the Naval Air Warfare Center, Weapons Division at Point Mugu. The 14,562 acres (58.93 km^2 or 22.753 sq. mi) island is currently controlled by the United States Navy and used as a weapons testing and training facility. The island has a 10,000-foot runway, communications, and mock cities for urban warfare training. Currently manned by two hundred Navy personnel, the island would require minimal changes to create a new country. Also, climate data for San Nicolas Island ranges from approximately forty degrees as a low to one hundred degrees during the hottest time of the summer, similar to Florida.

Third, we will divide the island into the Navy-held portion and the new country called 'Sanctuary.' The island would be equivalent to Haiti and The Dominican Republic, which share the same island but are two distinct sovereign states.

Fourth, just like Guantanamo Bay in Cuba, Sanctuary residents do not have the guaranteed constitutional rights of United States Citizens. Once removed and transferred to Sanctuary, they fall under that government and its laws.

Fifth, we will not create or enforce any laws or regulations on Sanctuary. The residents will be responsible for the creation and enforcement of all laws. Like any other sovereign state, they are responsible for what is legal or not on their land.

Sixth, we will wall off the naval area along with the landing strip, which will remain under the control of the Navy. We will create a single port of entry to accept new residents, food supplies, and building materials for them to develop their new country.

Seventh, no one can transport pets as they cannot deposit them on the island. For example, the ordinary housecat was one of the greatest threats to the island's wildlife and was eradicated by the Humane Society of the United States in 2009.

Eight, this is not a prison. The residents can move anywhere they like within the borders defined as their country, Sanctuary. The United States will supply them with building materials, tools, fuel, and food supplies under the foreign aid program.

Ninth, construction of the wall and other housing will begin within the next one hundred and twenty days from the release and approval of this memo.

Tenth, the island's west side will be ceded or given to the new country of Sanctuary by the Navy.

The seven-man congressional committee, four democrats and three republicans, began the meeting with one item on the agenda: to put plan 'B' into motion. The Plan 'B' would be modeled after the Guantanamo Bay detention camp in Cuba. It would include the creation of a new illegal immigrant homeland location outside the Constitution's reach and removing the many legal challenges faced on United States soil.

Since the immigrant's country of origin refused to allow them to return, the committee would create a new country to deport them to. The black project fund would supply money for the 'new country' without official accounting. The committee would replace U.S. Immigration and Customs Enforcement (I.C.E.) with a secret group of undercover agents. Sanctuary cities would be challenged directly and brushed aside quietly by any means necessary. The details of this dark project will only be revealed to a few selected members of Congress and Senate. Even the President would be unaware of plan 'B' to avoid executive order intervention. An illegal immigrant would be detained, collected by the undercover agents, and listed as deported when questioned by anyone. Once 'deported to Sancturay,' any remaining legal procedures would be logged as a no-show defendant.

The first question from the committee was, 'What if someone is murdered or killed on Sanctuary Island?' Congressman Harris looked up from the paperwork he was reading and addressed this question slowly. "The laws of the sovereign State of Sancturay will govern the penalty. The United States has no jurisdiction over a sovereign state and will take no action. The United States laws or law enforcement does not have jurisdiction and can not intervene."

The next question followed: 'What if they find a way off the island?' "Well," started Mr. Harris. 'The island is sixty-one miles off the coast of California. The area is heavily patrolled and would be challenging to navigate in a boat. Unlike the prison in Alcatraz, which is only one and a quarter miles from San Francisco, Sanctuary is fifty times as far. It is not likely to be undertaken and completed successfully."

Congressman Smith sat back in his chair, arms folded with disbelief written all over his face. He spoke slowly and chose his words carefully. "Why would these sanctuary cities hand over these people to us if they won't hand them over to I.C.E.?" Mr. Harris was waiting and prepared for this question. "I have been in constant contact with the mayors and other officials controlling these so-called sanctuary cities. Most agree it was a terrible mistake, but they cannot return because of political pressures. They are looking for an out to clean up their cities but cannot call I.C.E. according to the sanctuary agreement they committed to. We are not I.C.E.; in fact, we don't even exist. Should our agents arrive and take these people into custody, there is no violation of their agreement as a sanctuary city. Furthermore, they have agreed to 'drop a dime' on these bad apples and give us time to get there and remove them with our people, not I.C.E."

Congresswoman Martin, the only female on the committee, spoke up. "Well," she started, "we grab these people, and then what? Won't someone start looking to see what happened to them?" Mr. Harris leaned forward and folded his hands before speaking. "The people we are removing are gang members, rapists, child predators, murderers, and other significant felons. We are not after the people with parking tickets or stealing candy bars. We want the people who are dangerous to the community. I would find it hard to believe that a fellow gang member would call up and look for one of his friends as that would possibly target them. The standard answer to use is that they must have been deported. Please check with the consulate from where they came from for more information. Remember, they are here illegally and untrackable by anyone, government or private individual. Finally, if the states charge a severe crime and imprison someone, after their release, they are deported to the country of origin or the country of Sanctuary by our agents. Either way, they are out of the United States, which will help relieve our country's crisis."

Congressman Harris calls for a vote of the committee. "If you all favor going forward with Plan 'B,' raise your hand." Each member looked at the other and slowly raised their hand, accepting the proposed Plan 'B' and moving it forward from the committee. "Thank you," replied Mr. Harris. "Please leave all the memos on the table before you; this meeting never happened. Enjoy the rest of your day." He ended, stood up, and left the room.

San Nicolas Island

Ten days after the meeting, which never took place, a small team of five officials landed at San Nicolas' airfield. The documents they carried directed the Officer in charge, Captain Miller, to take them to the Commander of the Navy base. While the Captain requested a transport vehicle, he noticed the airplane they arrived on had no identification numbers on the tail. Strange, he thought. When the transport arrived, the five officials and the Navy personnel headed toward the command building in Nicktown, a half mile away. The trip was without verbal communication or explanation of their visit. Upon arrival, they exited the transport and were directed into the main building, disappearing through the large glass door to await the base commander. The transport driver gave the Captain a look that one could only describe as 'holy shit – what is that about' as they climbed back into the transport and drove away.

The Commander arrived about ten minutes after the five officials entered the building, and the five men were ushered into the Commander's office by the duty officer. The Commander assumed his place in an oversized chair behind his desk, and the five men formed a semi-circle around the front of the desk, each in a wooden chair. Commander Johnstone spoke first. "And what may I attribute this visit to gentleman?" He asked. The man in the center chair opened a small briefcase and handed the Commander a stack of official papers. As the Commander took the papers being pushed across the desk by the man, he requested the names of those with whom he was meeting. The man in the center who had passed the papers spoke lowly, "We are just messengers, and our names are irrelevant. Please read the documents."

Commander Johnstone picked up the papers and began reading, stopping as he went and voicing what was on the documents. "It says here you intend to land personnel and equipment on this island and build a wall." The Commander glanced up, and the five men's faces were without expression. He continued, "And the Navy will remove all military equipment from the island's western side. This is a tall order for my men to pick up and move everything on this island to the east side. It would take some time to accomplish it, and you have not even told me why we are doing it." The man in the center looked to his left and right before speaking, considering the other four men seated before the large desk. "Your orders are in the documents, Sir. We have presented you with all you need to know to complete the mission. Anything else is above your rank and classified. You do understand me, Sir?" Commander Johnstone looked directly at the five men sitting before him. He could tell by their blank expressions that they meant what they said and spoke timidly. "Well, how long do we have to complete this task?" Once again, the man in the center replied. "It is all in the documents, but you must complete it within thirty days. Our people will be here in ten days to start our part of the mission. And by the way, suspend all Navy leaves for the next ninety days as of today."

The meeting ended as quickly as it began. Commander Johnstone was left totally in the dark as to why, but being a Navy officer, he was determined to complete his mission. The transport picked up the five men, and they left the island in the same plane that had brought them there. To an outsider, one would believe the encounter and meeting never happened.

Commander Johnstone reviewed the documents after dinner that evening. He was a veteran of different operations, but this was, at best, far afield from anything he had performed in the past. He thought of verifying the documents through Washington; that would be his main call to Admiral Lisa Franchetta at the Pentagon the next day.

As he entered his office the following day, he stopped before the Officer on duty's desk. "Lieutenant, get me Admiral Lisa Franchetta on the secure phone line at the Pentagon; I'll take it on my office phone." The Lieutenant looked up quickly before replying, "The Pentagon, Sir?" Johnstone turned and stopped before speaking, "Yes, Lieutenant, Admiral Lisa Franchetta at the Pentagon, do I need to repeat it?" "No, Sir!" replied the Lieutenant.

Commander Johnstone entered his office and dropped into his oversized chair behind his desk. The voice of the Lieutenant followed a knock on the door, "The Pentagon is on the line, sir." The Commander looked at the phone, trying to put together how to approach the previous day's events. He picked up the telephone's receiver and spoke softly. "Admiral?" "Yes, Commander, this is Admiral Franchetta," was the reply. She continued, "And what may I attribute this call to, sir?" The Commander took a deep breath before speaking, "Well, Admiral, yesterday, an envoy of five men arrived at San Nicolas Island with a sealed packet of documents. The documents are a directive instructing me to..." "Stop," echoed the Admiral over the phone. "I do not want to hear what is in the documents." Followed without a pause. "But Admiral," replied the Commander. Again, the Admiral stopped him mid-sentence. "Commander, let me make this clear. I do not know what is in the alleged packet. Your job, Commander, is to execute missions to their completion. If, for some reason, you can not do your job, I will have you reassigned and put someone there who can complete the mission. Do I need to have you reassigned?" "No, Admiral." The Commander replied. "Do your job, Commander, and as for this call, I have not spoken with you about anything. Have a good day, Commander." And the Admiral hung up the phone.

The Commander knew whatever was going on was above the Admiral's rank. He reopened the packet of documents and began laying out a plan to achieve the mission. Damn, he thought, this is going to take every man on this base to complete. I've got thirty days to complete a three-month mission. "Lieutenant!" yelled the Commander. The door opened quickly with the Lieutenant standing within its frame. "I want all staff officers in the briefing room in fifteen minutes. And I mean all, no excuses." The Lieutenant replied with a solid "Yes, Sir!" and left the room.

The briefing started with the Commander planning to move all Navy communication sites, weapons, spent munitions, and weapon test equipment from the island's western side. Everything needed to be moved and reinstalled on the island's east side. The officers in the room looked at each other as if any one of them had a reason for the action. With none found, Warrant Officer Clark raised his hand and stood up. "Sir, is there a reason for moving all Navy equipment from the island's west side and clearing it of all munitions?" The Commander paused before answering, "The Environmental Protection Agency wants the island cleaned up." Warrant Officer Clark hesitated for a moment before replying. "What the E.P.A., Sir?" Johnstone looked directly at Officer Clark, saying. "That's right, the E.P.A. Does that answer your question, Sir?" The Warrant Officer responded as he sat down quickly, "Yes, Sir!"

The Commander continued, "We have only thirty days to complete this, and non-military personnel will work on other projects on the island. There will be no communication between Navy staff and non-military personnel, and I do not want to hear any scuttlebutt about what they are doing. All Navy personnel are to work on the projects I have laid out, and I have canceled all leave as of today for the next ninety days. You have two hours to gather your teams and equipment from the motor pool and start this project. I suggest extended hours each day to speed up the project. At this time, I am taking no questions." With that stated, the Commander picked up his papers and left the room.

As requested, each Officer gathered the needed Navy personnel and equipment and moved to the island's western side. Breaking the island into small block areas, the men could clear the area quickly. Communication equipment was dismantled, moved to the island's east side, and reassembled and re-certified. The men gathered the spent munitions and piled them up as scrap metal. Ten days into the cleanup project, the Navy men turned their attention to the mock city where the military trained for urban combat. As per their orders, the buildings were repaired and secured. None of the Navy personnel questioned the Commander's orders and accepted the reality of some good reason for doing what they were doing, whatever that may be.

On day eleven, change was in the air as C5-Galaxy heavy-lift cargo planes filled the blue sky above the island. They looked like a swarm of giant birds descending on a sandy beach as they landed on the ten-thousand-foot airstrip on the island. Each C5 landed in perfect order as if choreographed for a dance. They taxied to an area before the sizeable hangar and came to rest, holding a perfect line. The Navy's field officer was responsible for issuing clearance to land for each and recorded how many aircraft were on the field. The final count of aircraft came to seventeen, seventeen C5 Galaxys, and none with identification markings. The Officer stood wondering where someone could acquire seventeen military airplanes and fly them without markings. The Officer approached the plane closest to his position, where an armed guard greeted him. "Sorry, Sir, this is now a restricted area. Please leave here at once." The only words spoken by the armed man who, while saying the words, raised and pointed his rifle at the Navy officer. The one thing the

Navy officer knew was that this person, whoever he was, meant business, and he complied without uttering a word.

C5 Galaxy with No Markings

The field Officer decided to take a position well away from the aircraft. From that location, he just stood quietly and watched. As soon as all the aircraft parked in the area before the single large hangar, the first plane in line moved forward. The side door opened, followed by the cargo doors, front and rear. About fifteen men exited the short stairs of the plane and moved into groups. Some men wore green, and others camouflage or a combination of green and camouflage. They looked like military personnel, but no identification was visible. There were no name tags, rank symbols, or anything about who these people were. Like the Galaxy itself, there are no markings anywhere.

C5 Galaxy Being Unloaded

They unloaded trucks, temporary housing, equipment, and construction vehicles from the first plane. When the men unloaded the Galaxy, they hitched all the equipment together and started the trip down the lone road heading to the island's west side. The Galaxy remained long enough to secure the loading doors and exits fired its engines, and accelerated down the runway for takeoff. The plane's wheels barely left the pavement when the second Galaxy took its place and began to unload. Again, about fifteen men dressed the same as the first group exited the plane and began work unloading the aircraft. The heavy equipment varied in size and purpose, but all related to building something big. As soon as the Galaxy was unloaded, like the first group of men, they hitched up and drove the equipment toward the island's west side.

The second Galaxy secured its doors, fired its engines, and headed down the runway, following the first plane to exit.

The routine of unloading the planes continued for hours. One Galaxy at a time moved into position and was unloaded by the men aboard the aircraft. Strangely, none of the men spoke while unloading. The men knew what they needed to do and did it without saying anything. Whoever they were, the men were highly trained professionals. The Field Officer's only thoughts were, professional at what?

After dark, they finished unloading the last of the Galaxys. The Field Officer watched the men work all day, looking for some indication of who they were. He watched the final plane's bright lights turn on and start down the runway, disappearing into the night, and the men and equipment travel down the road until they were out of sight. He slowly walked out to where the day's events had taken place. Other than some scrapes on the pavement, there was no sign of what or who was there. He looked down the single road leading west, closed his eyes, and thought, could I have dreamed all of this? I think I just witnessed over two hundred and fifty men unload seventeen C5 Galaxys and disappear down the only road leading to the island's west side. He would say it was impossible if he did not witness it for himself. He remembered what the Commander said: "No scuttlebutt" about what was happening. He turned and walked toward his vehicle to leave the field. While walking, he said, "Since I don't know what I saw, I must have not seen anything. At least, there is nothing I want to talk about. I would have been better off spotting a flying saucer. At least someone would believe that."

For the next twenty days, Navy personnel scoured the island's northwest side, collecting munitions and experimental launcher equipment. The weapons test area was in the final cleanup phase, and Navy staff transported the last of the precision radar systems to the island's east side. As the Navy personnel looked south from the testing range, they could see clouds of dust and the smoke of diesel engines. Whatever the visitors were doing, it continued from early morning to after dark and must be an extensive project.

On day number thirty-one, the C5 Galaxys returned. They repeated the same routine the first time they arrived, landing and lining up in front of the large hangar. One by one, they were unloaded by men on board the plane. The men removed semi-trucks preloaded with large fence panels and other fencing hardware from the belly of the Galaxys. The Field Officer remembered seeing these panels before. They were the "Trump border wall panels" that had arrived on San Nicholas Island. Just as before, the trucks drove down the single road leading west and disappeared. Once the men cleared each

Galaxy of its cargo, it left the island, returning to some unknown air facility.

The Galaxys returned daily with semi-truck loads and border wall panels for thirty days. The only change in the routine was that the truck drivers returned from the island's west side with an unloaded truck, and they transferred to the loaded truck and traveled once again down the road to the island's west side. Then, the Galaxys swallowed up the empty trucks to make a return trip. The field officer tried to estimate how much of the border wall had been transported to the island. After checking the fence dimensions on the Internet and counting the number of trucks unloaded, he estimated that the wall would be over ten miles long. Damn, he thought, that's enough wall to run the island's entire length from north to south.

After the border wall was delivered, the Galaxys returned with loaded semi-trucks, this time loaded with building materials and trailers. The trailers were the type you would expect to find in a trailer park. Over the following weeks, hundreds of trailers and enough building materials to build a small city arrived. The field officer also noticed that the load on one truck consisted of construction tools and equipment. While he sat in his office, his mind began to wander. Closing his eyes, he imagined a fully stocked Home Depot or Lowes constructed on the island's west side.

Curiosity finally overtook the Field Officer. Climbing a ladder to the top of the large hangar gives him a view of some of the island's western side. He directs his attention to the west with his plane spotter binoculars in hand. He could now view a large wall under construction as far as he could see. And behind the wall were new buildings. A small city surrounded by trailers was being constructed, like a trailer park in the middle of nowhere. As he scanned a little north, he could see large steel buildings, maybe warehouses. Scanning south, he could see the unmistakable smoke stacks of a power-generating plant. Whatever they were building, it was going to be self-sufficient. Whatever it was, it seemed to have everything. The visitors were changing an empty island into a small city with all the needed support right before his eyes.

Four days went by before the return of the Galaxys to the island. As before, they swarmed the isle like a flock of birds before landing and depositing their cargo. The semi-trucks, this time, were all loaded with large pipes and plumbing fixtures. As before, the loaded semi-trucks were removed from the planes and replaced by the unloaded trucks from the island's west side. And as before, after being unloaded and reloaded, each Galaxy departed the island to places unknown.

During this time, the wall construction was advancing by the hour, and the wall was now visible less than a half mile from the field's runway. It appeared to be over thirty feet tall, with flat metal sheets on the top to prevent it from being scaled. It was a challenging barrier isolating the east and west sides of the island.

Island Border Wall

Two days later, the Galaxys returned once again. This time, the planes carried large tanks for the storage of liquids. Each tank was painted a different color to identify its contents when filled. The field officer speculated the green/white tanks were for water, the yellow/black tanks were for fuel oil, and the brown/white tanks were designated propane. And like all the materials transported to the island by the Galaxys, they were transported to the island's west side by the semi-trucks. Still, the Field Officer had no idea what they could be constructing beside the large wall from the airport runway in his purview.

It was about three months into the project that the unknown construction crew were in the process of performing, and the first signs of their mission became apparent. The wall stopped abruptly on each side of the road leading to the island's west side. The unknown construction crew that arrived on the Galaxys had constructed two large electric gates around fifty feet apart, converting the missing section of the wall into what looked like a port of entry. They displayed a sizeable sign over the west side gate: "Welcome to The Republic of Sanctuary." The only question that remained was, what the hell is "The Republic of Sanctuary?"

During the next two weeks, the road leading west was paved using the Navy's runway equipment and signage in English and Spanish indicating where you were along the roadway to Sanctuary.

The greatest surprise came one week later when the Galaxys landed again loaded with E.V. cars. As before, the vehicles were loaded on transport trucks, traveled through the gates to Sanctuary, and returned an hour later empty to be reloaded on the Galaxys to leave the island. The best count the Field Officer could get was at least two hundred small electric cars dropped off somewhere for something. The last Galaxy carried a small white electric bus marked "Transportation" on both sides.

Ninety days after the unknown construction crew arrived, the C5 Galaxys returned for the last time. A long parade of equipment and men travel the road east and through the gates from Sanctuary. The equipment and men loaded into the Galaxys, and the plane departed when each one was to capacity. As the last of the men and equipment passed through the gates, the gates closed for the final time. Within one hour, the last of the Galaxys left the island, leaving no trace of anyone ever being there.

Whatever happened during the time the unknown construction crew was on the island was not known to Navy personnel. The only thing that remained was that the island was now divided into two parts: the Navy base of operations on the east side and the Republic of Sanctuary on the west. And as the Commander ordered, there was no scuttlebutt concerning what, if anything, had been done on the island.

A week later, the seven congressperson committee that put Plan 'B' into motion boarded a United Airlines flight from Washington, DC, to Los Angeles, California. From there, they would board a private plane to transport them to San Nicolas Island. The official reason for the visit was to see the Navy Operations on an average day to make recommendations for future funding. The real reason was to make a "flyover of The Republic of Sanctuary" to see what they had authorized to be created under cover of a "black Operation Project, Plan 'B'." The committee would document Sanctuary in photos with cameras in their carry-on luggage.

Sitting aboard the United flight, they felt satisfied that they had created a new country without a trace linking it back to them. The paperwork transferring the western part of the island was already before the Chief of Staff at the Pentagon and would be signed and executed upon their return with the photos of the new country. The Republic of Sanctuary would be an official sovereign state by the end of the week, recognized by the United States as such.

Congressman Harris placed his briefcase on his knees and opened the locks. He reached inside and withdrew seven identical packets from the case. Congressman Harris gave each committee member a copy of the document to review and approve. The first page of the document follows:

Constitution of The Republic of Sanctuary

PREAMBLE

The Sanctuary people proclaim this Constitution:

To guarantee their inalienable and imprescriptible rights to life, liberty, and the pursuit of happiness, in accordance with their Act of Independence of 2023 and with the Universal Declaration of the Rights of Man of 1948.

To constitute a Sanctuarian nation, socially just, economically free, and politically independent.

To establish a stable and strong state that protects the values, traditions, sovereignty, independence, and national vision.

To implant democracy, which implies ideological pluralism and political alternation, and to affirm the inviolable rights of the Sanctuarian People.

To fortify the national unity, eliminating all discrimination between the populations, of the towns and the countryside, by the acceptance of the community of languages and of culture and by the recognition of the right to progress, to information, to education, to health, to work and to leisure for all citizens [masculine] and citizens [feminine].

To assure the separation and the harmonious division of the powers of the State to the service of the fundamental interests and priorities of the Nation.

To establish a governmental regime based on fundamental liberties and the respect for human rights, social peace, economic equity, the equity of gender, concerted action, and the participation of all the population in the grand decisions engaging the national life by an effective decentralization.

To ensure women's representation in the instances of power and decision, it must conform to the equality of the sexes and equity of gender.

TITLE I. THE REPUBLIC OF SANCTUARY

ITS EMBLEM AND ITS SYMBOLS

CHAPTER I. The Republic of Sanctuary
First Article

Sanctuary is an indivisible, sovereign, independent, free, democratic, and unified Republic.

Page 1

The committee members sat back and began reading the "Constitution of Sanctuary," the country they were responsible for creating. After a short time, each member returned the documents to Mr. Harris and nodded in approval. Soon, a new sovereign country would come into existence with the stroke of a pen by the Pentagon's Chief of Staff. The how and why the country of Sanctuary came to be would be another conspiracy theory for someone to write a book about.

The five-and-a-half-hour flight from D.C. to Los Angeles went without event. The committee had a good lunch on the plane, followed by cocktails, adding some life to a boring flight across the country. After landing, a private pilot greeted the committee, who would ferry them to the island. They quickly boarded a ten-passenger twin-engine Cessna for the short trip to San Nicholas Island, each committee member positioning themselves into the best seats to take photos from the plane.

Transport Airplane

When the aircraft arrived over San Nicholas Island, Congressman Harris requested the pilot reduce his altitude and circle for pictures of the entire island.

The waters around the island were a deep blue, and dolphins swam in circles looking for food. Wave-cut terraces and windswept grassy hills define the island. The most prominent hill on the island seemed to be very tall compared to the surrounding areas. The pilot, eavesdropping on the committee conversation, pipes up, "That is Jackson Hill with an elevation of nine hundred and seven feet above sea level. While shaking his head, Congressman Harris leaned over to the man beside him before commenting. "How does the pilot know that kind of shit?" His fellow committee members shrugged his shoulders, "Got me." He replied.

As the plane circled the island, you could see a mid-sized new city on the island's western side. The island was divided into two parts by a tall wall, and it was clear that a newly installed road system had crisscrossed the area. They could see the large steel buildings and a power plant near the island's southern end. The pilot speaks up again. "The Navy must have been busy here. Six months ago, this was a barren island." Congressman Harris calls up to the pilot. "A few more passes, please. We want to get more pictures of the place before we land."

The pilot circled the island for almost a half hour before being instructed to land on the airfield. The plane taxied up to the large single hangar and came to a stop. "Here you are, folks, San Nicholas Island." Ejected from his mouth. The pilot lowered the stairs, and the committee members exited the plane in single file. The Field Officer waited at the bottom of the stairs and greeted each committee member by name, unquestionably well-rehearsed.

They could see the tall steel wall and two gates across the landing field. Playing dumb, Congressman Harris asks the Field Officer about the existence of the wall and gates. The Officer shakes his head while speaking, "Not sure, Sir. The sign on the other side says Republic of Sanctuary; that is all I can tell you, Sir." That information was precisely what Congressman Harris was hoping to hear. The less people knew about what had occurred, the better it was for everyone involved. "Thank you, Officer," Mr Harris replied.

Two transport vehicles arrived to move the committee members to the Nicktown headquarters. The short trip took only a few minutes, and the committee arrived at a large building and entered through the glass doors. A lieutenant stood up from behind the desk he was sitting at inside the front door. "We were expecting you, and the Commander will see you in his office momentarily," Flowed from his mouth. Within seconds, the door to the Commander's office opened, and the Commander stood there smiling and waving for the committee to come into his office. As the committee entered, they were seated in seven soft plush chairs before the Commander's desk. The Commander moved around the desk and slowly settled into his oversized chair.

Congressman Harris begins the conversation. "You have done a great job, Sir, and we are impressed with the work you have achieved here on the island." The Commander smiles before saying, "Thank you, and I hope I can continue with whatever Congress needs to get done here, whatever that may be." Mr. Harris glances left and right at the other committee members before continuing. "The committee knows no one has told you much about what was happening here on the island. And the details are still minimal at this time. Here is what we can say to you as of today. The United States Border Control staff will arrive on this island in about two weeks. Their mission will be to install electronic sensors, lighting, and other detection equipment along the length of the wall. This island will be shared by the country of The Republic of Sanctuary and treated like Mexico's border. Your Navy staff will continue as before with your duties, and the Border Control staff will construct living quarters needed along the wall and stop any illegal immigration onto the east side of the island. Navy personnel should not attempt to travel into Sanctuary, and we would appreciate limiting gossip between the Navy and Border Control Staff. We don't need a lot of unfounded stories getting back to the mainland, now do we?" The Commander replies, "No Sir, we do not need gossip circulating here on this base or back home."

Mr. Harris continues, "For our part here today, I believe the committee can be generous in recommending additional funding for your staff and operations of this facility, provided you keep everything under control. Maybe new living quarters and recreational facilities on the base. Need to make our Navy people happy, now don't we." The Commander leans forward before speaking, "I am sure that will make the Navy happy, and trust me, I will make sure there will be no scuttlebutt from my staff, Sir."

Mr. Harris rises from his chair and says, "That is what we wanted to hear from you, Commander, and I will relay that message to Washington. Expect the Border Control staff in two weeks, and please, there will be no gossip on or off this island." The entire committee stood, and the Commander shook each of their hands, sealing the deal.

The Commander called out to the Lieutenant to alert the transport vehicles that the committee was ready to leave, and the Congressional committee was boarding the aircraft within minutes to exit the island. As the twin-engine Cessna lifted off the runway, the Field Officer looked over to the Navy transport drivers before speaking. "That was the shortest visit in history. I hope nothing went wrong." One of the drivers replied, "The congressmen were all smiling; I think they were happy. But then, what the hell do I know."

About two weeks later, the first border agents landed on a rainy Tuesday morning in a small plane on the base. Captain Miller, the Field Officer on duty, greeted them. "Good morning, and welcome to the San Nicholas Island Navy base." Said Captain Miller, reaching out his hand to shake theirs. Each of the six border agents shook the Captain's hand as they walked past him and stood waiting. The Senior Border Agent spoke after the greeting. "Captain, we will require a Navy vehicle to survey the wall built across the island. Something enclosed would be great with all this rain, but we will take whatever you can supply if necessary." The Captain smiled, saying, "I have just what you need. All enclosed, all-wheel drive will go almost anywhere on this island. Never been stuck yet with this baby." "That would be perfect, Captain." Replied the agent. "Step inside the hangar, and I will get it for you." The Captain replies as he turns and walks away.

The Captain returns, driving an H2 Hummer from the rear of the hangar. As the vehicle came to a stop, the Senior agent spoke up, "Captain, exactly where did the Navy acquire the Hummer?" "Well, sir." The Captain started, "You see, sir, it is a long story of how this Hummer got here on the island, sir." The Senior agent stopped the Captain right there. "I don't think I want to know how it got here and assigned to the Navy. But it will work out great for what we need to do. Thank you." The six border agents climbed into the Hummer, all shaking their heads and laughing. A civilian H2 Hummer on the Navy base was quite a surprise, and they could not wait to see what other surprises they would find.

2004 H2 Hummer

The border agents drive directly to the south end of the island. Once there, they turned north and began a slow ride along the newly constructed wall, making notes. They stopped constantly marking the coordinates of their handheld G.P.S., transferring notes to a map they brought. Some markings indicated future lighting, others electronic surveillance, other camera postpositions, and locations of needed buildings for their equipment and housing of personnel. They paid particular attention to the ends of the wall that stretched into the ocean. That area would be the most difficult to maintain, and they determined to mount equipment on a string of O.P.T. buoy-based offshore surveillance solutions running parallel to the wall and along the western perimeter of the island to protect those areas. Unlike the Mexican border, this border would be secure and closed. Anyone attempting to leave Sanctuary by land or sea would trigger an alarm.

The trip covering the island took most of the day to complete. They returned to the Navy hangar with detailed maps and notes in their hand and once again greeted the Captain. As the agents exited the Hummer, the Senior Agent said, "Thank you, Captain, for using the Hummer and your cooperation today. Please inform the Commander that additional construction staff will arrive within the week to construct the buildings and install the needed equipment here on the island for the assigned agents.

Also, shortly, supplies will be delivered by Army personnel to The Republic of Sanctuary under the Foreign Aid Act. I know this seems unusual, but the Army will require it to do it this way. Foreign Aid will continue into the foreseeable future and should not be interfered with. Thank you again, Captain."

The border agents boarded the small plane and were airborne within minutes, disappearing to the east. The Captain promptly traveled to the base headquarters and relayed the detailed message presented to him by the senior agent to the Commander. The Captain turned and left the Commander's office after delivering the message. The Commander sat back in his oversized office chair, trying to grasp what was happening. Whatever the game plan, he was not privy to it and felt left out, almost as if he, the Commander, was not trusted to know what they were doing.

Almost a week went by before the first cargo transport planes arrived. The first thing the Flight Line Officer, Captain Miller, noted was that these planes displayed clear markings of the Air Force. He quickly identified the markings, starkly contrasting with the other Galaxy aircraft that arrived months earlier and had no marking.

U.S. Airforce C5 Galaxy

The aircraft arrived two at a time. Before the large hangar, the planes taxied to the area and opened the doors to unload their cargo. Air Force personnel meticulously removed the contents from each cargo bay and transported the containers to where the gates in the border wall were. The containers were marked on both sides with the content they contained. Captain Miller could identify many containers holding electronic equipment and exterior lighting. He then identified containers marked with O.P.T. Offshore Surveillance Buoy Solution. Captain Miller was unsure what they were but knew what a buoy was. He thought, how can a buoy floating in the ocean surveil something? Well, whether or not they could surveil something or not there were a lot of them.

The following day, two more cargo aircraft arrived and continued piling containers along with the others from the previous day. On the third day, an Army personnel plane landed early in the morning, and over one hundred

Army staff members exited the plane. Within an hour, another Galaxy landed. It carried equipment for moving the containers and construction. The Army staff divided into groups and began repositioning the containers. Once the men had the containers realigned, they opened them and put the equipment on wooden pallets on the ground. Large forklifts picked up the pallets and shuttled the material along different wall areas.

At one point, the Army opened one of the containers holding the surveillance buoys. Captain Miller could see this buoy, which was nothing he had seen in the past. A sheet of paper that blew away from the crate containing one of the buoys moved close to where Captain Miller was standing. The Captain walked over quickly to intercept the paper, stopping its advance. Picking the paper up, he found a photo detailing equipment installed on the buoy. My God, he thought as he reviewed the paperwork. These things are a floating armed communications center with onboard power generation used for surface surveillance and security monitoring of offshore areas. What or who will they monitor on a mostly abandoned island off the coast of California? The second page of the paperwork gave a detailed description of the buoy's capabilities. It read in part: One system can monitor more than 1,600 sq mi (4,144 sq km) of ocean surface on a permanent or temporary basis, with the ability to link multiple surveillance assets together over large ocean areas, giving end-users visibility into potentially damaging environmental or illegal activities.

O.P.T. Surveillance Buoy Layout

The Captain carried the paper he recovered to where it had started its flight in the wind. Handing it to a Private opening another container, he smiled and said, "I don't know if you need this, but I caught it blowing down the runway." "Thank you, Sir." The Private replied as the Captain turned and headed back toward the large hangar.

The Captain estimated by the number of containers marked "Surveillance Buoy" that they had enough to encircle a large part, if not all, of the island. The Captain's mind ran riot with crazy ideas about what was happening on the island's west side, with the Commander's words echoing in his head: no scuttlebutt.

The Captain's walk back toward the hangar was interrupted with a single thought in his head. How will they get those buoys from where they are along the wall now three miles to the other side of the island? Maybe they planned to move them by truck to the island's shore, onto a boat, and locate and anchor them from there? That, he thought, would take forever to complete. Then he thought, it's not his problem and above his rank.

The Captain's answer to how they would install the buoys came three days later, with three Army heavy lift helicopters appearing in the early morning sky over the airfield.

Heavy Lift Helicopters

The helicopters briefly landed, and the crew on board deployed lifting harnesses. They lifted off, attached, and headed off to the island's west side with a buoy hanging below, each to be deployed along the island's west coast.

While the helicopters were installing the buoys, other Army men were installing lighting and communication towers along the entire length of the wall. Still, other Army men were erecting prefab buildings. Some buildings appeared to be for housing, others for storage, and one looked like an equipment repair building or shop. Two weeks later, the Army added two additional buildings along the wall, and they appeared to be a mess hall to eat and a commissary for supply purchases. A week later, the Army erected two more buildings on the west side of the large gates. As you would pass through the gates, the buildings were around fifty feet inside. Whatever they were building was a significant long-term facility.

Other C5 Galaxys transported materials to the island almost daily during construction. Some unloaded containers remained along the wall, while the Army transported others through the double gates to the island's west side.

After months of building whatever it was, the Army packed up the troops and left the island. The fully stocked buildings sat empty. The installed lighting along the wall glowed every night, and no soul occupied the encampment. Whatever they built was complete and needed only someone to take possession.

Three weeks passed before the coming of the souls to take ownership of the small town the Army constructed. About a hundred border patrol agents exited two Air Force aircraft, and, without a word, they were transported the short distance to their new home. Captain Miller could see from the field office the men moving their belongings from the aircraft into the housing areas constructed. Well, the Captain thought to himself, whatever it is must finally be coming to life.

Over the next week, a small number of other border agents arrived. It appeared to the Captain they were the ranking agents. Like the other agents, they migrated their belongings into the living quarters and disappeared. The Captain could see from the airfield the agents were busy checking out the installed equipment along the wall. The agents moved back and forth all day, and not once did one of the agents travel over to the Navy base and introduce themselves, not once.

It was Friday, and the Captain looked forward to a weekend off. The activity along the wall seemed never to stop. In a moment of weakness, the Captain grabbed his field glasses and directed them to the wall area. The Captain could see the Border Agents unpacking one of the last containers. He adjusted the focus to see what it contained. What is that, he thought. What the hell is that? Is it a container of signs? He stood motionless for a short time. That is what they are signs. He waited to read the writing on the large sign. Finally, the sign came into view. The four-foot by four-foot, white signs with bright red lettering read in English, "U.S. Military Base. No Travel Beyond This Point ALLOWED. Failure To Comply

Will Result in the Use Of Deadly Force. KEEP Back For Your Safety." The message on the sign was repeated in Spanish, Arabic, French, and Chinese.

He watched as the signs were taken through the gates by Border Agents into The Republic of Sanctuary and systematically mounted to the wall about every five hundred feet, making it clear not to attempt to wander past the wall. The only question that Captain Miller now had was who was there to walk past the damn wall. The Border Agents must know that the island's west side has no population. The Captain moved into the small office in the large hangar and sat slowly into his chair. He leaned back and closed his eyes, thinking, "What has God or the Devil brought to San Nicolas Island?"

CHAPTER SEVEN

Citizens of Sanctuary

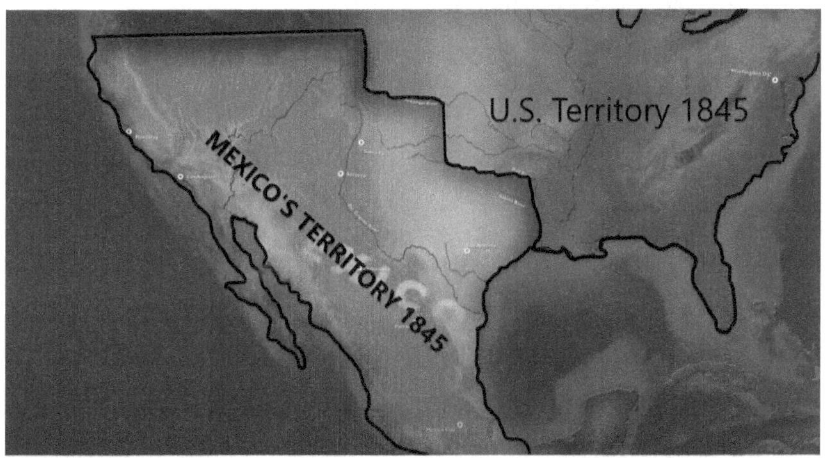

Congressman Harris called the final underground meeting at his Washington, D.C. home two weeks after the committee's flyover survey of The Republic of Sanctuary. When everyone arrived, he pointed to a large dining room at the end of the hall. As the seven-person committee moved into the dining room and sat down, excitement was in the air. The secret project they had been working on for many months was finally complete.

As you entered the room, a large, long table appeared surrounded by black chairs. Once inside, you first notice that Congressman Harris had pictures of his deceased wife and daughter carefully placed on the long mantle over the single fireplace. The only things remaining of the two most prominent people in Congressman Harris's life were a few photos and their memories.

The committee moved around the table, and each member sat to hear the latest update on the project. While sitting at the end of the table, Congressman Harris looked around the room, reached out with his right hand, and waved a thumbs-up sign signaling success. The committee gave a sign of relief, and congratulations flowed. They successfully executed Plan 'B' to completion without intervention from government oversight. After briefly shaking hands and cheering, "We did it," Mr. Harris called the meeting to order to present a final summary of the secret project.

With his head looking down, Mr. Harris began to speak, "It seems like this adventure took forever to complete. I can't tell you how many times I walked down the halls of the Congressional building expecting someone to point a finger at me, screaming 'He did it,' with the F.B.I. in tow. You probably suffered the same experience during this long, drawn-out process. It has been challenging these last several months, but we have finally reached the end of our journey. Two days ago, the Navy Secretary signed over the San Nicolas Island land to the Republic of Sanctuary. Thanks to the good people sitting here tonight, the Republic of Sanctuary is now and forever sovereign. The only sad thing this evening is that this project only came to be because of the murder of my daughter." Mr. Harris stopped for a few moments to collect himself. "Rest in peace, honey; this creation was all for you." As he finished the sentence.

Mr. Harris continues, "We must consider and implement some final details here tonight. It is a little long, but please bear with me. I took the liberty of selecting the transport aircraft to the island, a Boeing Max 737. I got a hell of a deal on it for obvious reasons. Besides, Boeing promised the doors and wheels would not come off if I purchased the plane." The committee members burst into a loud laugh. Mr. Harris raised his hand and continued, "I felt the verbal guarantee was important. The Boeing manufacturer is customizing the plane to include seat anchors on each seat to handcuff a person, and the pilot can black out the windows during the flight. The blacking out of the windows removes flight information from the people transported to the island. We plan to transport and board the guests at Buckley Air Force Base In Aurora, Colorado. Flying from Aurora will allow a delay in flight time, distorting the distance the guests have traveled. The flight path will be one-half hour past the island, where the pilot will unblock the windows for five minutes, giving a clear view of only the Pacific Ocean. The goal is to disorient the guests as to where exactly they are. They will believe they have been moved thousands of miles over the ocean. The plane will make a slow turn and return to San Nicolas Island and land at the Navy air base. At the air base, the guests will deplane, and the Border Patrol will transport them by small bus through the two gates dividing the island. We have built two small buildings just inside the western gate. The first building is for receiving and removing guests from the bus, and the second is for the new arrival information building. The information building is where the guests will receive the needed information about their new home or country. If desired, the guests are allowed to ask questions, and they will receive a printed layout of the Republic of Sanctuary detailing all available services or lack thereof. After the guests get their indoctrination at the information center, the Border Patrol will transport them to their new living quarters in the Republic of Sanctuary." Mr. Harris paused for questions.

A raised hand at the table meant there would be a question. Mr. Harris points in the direction of the raised hand. The committee member says, "Well, Sir, we will pick up the guest at Buckley, but how will they get there? We don't have the assistance of I.C.E., so how?" Mr. Harris looks down at the papers before replying, "If you look back at page number three of the initial plan, you will find we have created a version of I.C.E. to gather and transport the guests. I refer to them as the 'Black Ice.' group. The sanctuary cities refuse to work with I.C.E., but they have no restrictions on working with our own Black Ice people. Our Black Ice people will take custody of the guests and ensure they are safely transported wherever needed. Legally, there is no problem, as the people we are detaining already have orders of deportation from a court. They remain in the United States because I.C.E. can not get their hands on them. These people can not claim a legal violation because they have already gone through the system. As a side note, New York City and others have contacted me to get an update on when they can expect to begin turning over their problem children to us. What they tell their constituents and what they will do will be different. Our Black Ice people have all the authority to take their guests into custody, as passed in a Bill slipped through Congress six weeks ago. To make it simple, we are online and ready to go as of tonight." Mr. Harris waits for another hand with a question. After a few moments, Mr. Harris continues, "I do not see any more questions." As Mr. Harris looks around the room, he says, "One last thing before we leave tonight. As this will be our final meeting concerning The Republic of Sanctuary, I want to thank each of you for your loyal support. And one more thing: I plan to give the indoctrination talk to the first guests who arrive at the Republic of Sanctuary to honor my daughter. Thank you, and have a good night." Mr. Harris ended, and the committee picked up the papers they carried with them, again shook hands, and left Mr. Harris' home.

After everyone left his home for the evening, Mr. Harris returned to the dining room and addressed the silent photos of his loved ones. With tears in his eyes, he softly said, "I failed you guys once, and I will not fail you again." With that said, he turned, left the room, turned off the lights, and went to bed.

An old idiom states, "Good News Travels Fast and Bad News has Wings." In the case of The Republic of Sanctuary being completed and ready to accept guests, both phrases of that idiom are true simultaneously. The good news was that cities finally had a solution to the repeat illegal offenders. The bad news applies to the unlawful, illegal offenders being removed from the streets of our cities and put somewhere they cannot harm anyone anymore. To sum it up, these illegal offenders were about to find what they were searching for: a sanctuary place.

Mr. Harris called Homeland Security to establish a direct telephone line to the Black Ice group. The supervisor at the Washington office gave Congressman Harris no resistance and promised to have a number by the following morning. The number would be listed under the 'Cleaning Services' title and made available on a 24 – 7 basis to receive calls. The caller only needed to give the time and place for the services, and the Black Ice group would handle the rest. Calling for cleaning services did not interfere with the sanctuary status of any city or state, leaving a plausible denial that no one called I.C.E. and made a report.

Forty-eight hours later, the new 'Cleaning Services' line and the Black Ice group were ready to respond. Homeland Security distributed the number to every large city, democrat or republican, controlled. How long it would take before someone used the telephone line was answered the following day with a call from Chicago giving the time and place of an illegal walking free after committing multiple violent crimes. The first 'dime had been dropped' on an illegal predator.

The Colombian national strolled out of the courthouse with a big smile after being released on an appearance ticket; the Black Ice group took him into custody without incident. Law enforcement moved the detainee to the new Black Ice detention center in Florida for future proceedings. The only information supplied to family members was he was facing deportation, the standard response.

In New York City, on the same day, another violent illegal immigrant was picked up by the Black Ice group after an anonymous call for cleaning services. The Venezuelan national had been arrested twenty-seven times for robbery and assault and already had an I.C.E. detainer issued but not honored by the city of New York. The detainee's only words spoken were, "You can't do this. I know my rights," as the Venezuelan was cuffed and led away by the Black Ice group. He was also detained and transported by Law enforcement and moved to the new Black Ice detention center in Florida for future proceedings. The only information supplied to family members was he was facing deportation, the standard response.

In Los Angeles the following morning, the Black Ice group arrested a Haitian man arrested seven times for raping underage girls. I.C.E. had a retainer posted for several months attempting to apprehend this man. The sanctuary status of the city did not allow the I.C.E. team to be notified upon his release, and he continually walked free to assault again. And like all the rest, he was also detained and transported by Law enforcement and moved to the new Black Ice detention center in Florida for future proceedings. The only information supplied to family members was he was facing deportation, the standard response.

Congressman Harris stayed in contact with the elite Black Ice group almost daily. The Black Ice group adjusted its methods by acquiring the list of remaining I.C.E . detainers. With this list, they could move around the cities' streets and detain wanted gang members as they identified them. This method gave the Black Ice group a significant advantage as they did not need to wait for a court appearance to arrest individuals with open detainers. Congressman Harris learned of the Black Ice group's new method and readily approved it. His only regret was his committee failed to think of it.

It was no longer a question of whether they could accomplish the mission of removing the illegals who acted like animals; it was a question of how fast the detention center filled up.

The call to the Congressman came twenty-one days into the operation. The detention center was holding one hundred and twenty-eight people. It was time for this first group of detainees to find what they were seeking: a sanctuary. Arrangements were made for the trip to The Republic of Sanctuary the following Tuesday afternoon for all one hundred and twenty-eight seekers of freedom. Congressman Harris would be there to greet them and hand them the keys to the Republic of Sanctuary to do with it what they pleased.

It was nine A.M. on Tuesday morning when Congressman Harris boarded the flight from Washington to Los Angeles. The flight was about five and a half hours long, minus the three-hour difference in time zones. The plans were to meet on San Nicolas Island at around two P.M. pacific time, leaving a margin for error of almost an hour. The guests were being boarded and flown to Buckley Air Force Base In Aurora, Colorado, for refueling, and then the pilot would follow the flight plan laid out by the committee to the island.

The Congressman reviewed his notes on the flight, trying to decide what to say to the individuals. He was more than aware they were troubled people, but the safety of the citizens of the United States needed to come before their claimed rights. He wrote down sentences and then crossed them out. What do you say to someone placed on an island to isolate them from the public? Maybe you need to think like they do and just lay it out there as they would. No sugar coating, no sweet talk. You are here because of your actions; frankly, even the countries you came from have refused to take you back. With those thoughts in the Congressman's mind, he was ready to make his first address to confront pure evil.

The Congressman's flight arrived early, and he transferred his belongings to the smaller commuter plane that would take him to the island. On the smaller plane, he pressed his head back into the headrest and closed his eyes, again reviewing what he might say. He opened his eyes and stared out the window, looking into the blue waters of the Pacific Ocean. It appeared so peaceful that he wondered if his wife and daughter would have enjoyed it. He was awakened from his short daydream by the pilot's voice over the plane's speaker system, "We will be landing on San Nicolas Island in five minutes."

The Congressman could feel the plane's wheels bumping as they pressed on the Navy base runway. The bumping became slower as the aircraft came to a stop outside the large hangar. As always, the Navy's flight Officer, Captain Miller, greeted the Congressman, "Good to see you again, Sir. Do I need to call for transportation so you can see the Commander at the Navy Headquarters?" The Congressman paused before speaking, "No, thank you. I am here today for other business with the Border Patrol Office. They will take care of everything from this point on. And my plane will be parked here for a short time to take me back off the island. Please tell the pilot where he should park it out of your way. Oh, and one more thing: a Boeing 737 will arrive soon. Could you assist Border Patrol with moving to a safe location for its passengers to deplane? After they deplane, the aircraft will leave the base directly." The Captain smiled before replying, "As long as the doors and wheels stay on it, everything will work fine." Then, the Captain turned and walked towards his office in the large hangar. The Congressman stood momentarily, shook his head, and thought, "God, can't anyone leave poor Boeing alone?"

The Congressman could see activity across the large runway, and in minutes, a vehicle from the Border Patrol was en route to where he was standing. The Agent at the wheel stopped the car and exited to address the Congressman. "Good afternoon, sir. I will take you to the main office to rest until the other plane arrives. Please be careful and do not strike your head on the vehicle as you get in." The car with the Congressman on board moved slowly across the large runway and stopped in front of the new central office that housed the Border Patrol. The Congressman exited the vehicle, walked quickly to the office door, and entered. Once inside, he discovered the air to be cooler than the air outside. Unlike his office, everything looks to be in place and orderly. Maybe, he thought, they tidied the place up to impress him, and if that were the case, he was impressed.

He located a comfortable chair in one corner of the room and waited for the Agent in charge to arrive. A few minutes later, the Senior Patrol Agent opened the door and entered the room. The Agent approached the Congressman and said, "Sir, I am Agent Romero, at your service. Is there anything you need to make you more comfortable?" Congressman Harris smiled, "No, I do not need anything, thank you." Agent Romero replied, "I have been across the border preparing things for the new arrivals. We have stationed extra armed agents there in case we encounter any problems. The informational center is ready, and according to my officer of the day, the Boeing will be arriving in fifteen minutes. Have I missed anything, Sir?" The Congressman shook his head, thinking, 'Why can't we make Congress this efficient? The only thing Congress is good at is getting lunch.'

A door to an inter-office opened, and another agent stepped from within and spoke while addressing the Congressman, "Excuse me, Sir. I think you should come and see what they are now reporting on satellite news about that ship that collided with the Baltimore Bridge earlier today." The Congressman stood, walked into the small office, and sat before a small television. He pointed to the T.V. before requesting the Agent to turn up the volume to hear the report.

With a live picture of the destroyed bridge on the screen, a 'crawler displayed along the bottom of the screen stating: 'Officials say no evidence ship collision involved intentional terrorism,' while a voice overlay reported:

"Six construction workers are now presumed dead after the container ship Dail crashed into the Francis Scott Key Bridge in Baltimore in the early hours today. Authorities say the cargo ship suffered a complete power blackout as it approached the bridge, with its lights blinking out as it endured a complete loss of propulsion. Though the cause of the ship's power outage is still being investigated, authorities confirmed there's no evidence the tragedy was a result of terrorism. The Secretary of Homeland Security shared a post on X detailing the U.S. Coast Guard's ongoing search and rescue efforts. In his post, he said, "There are no indications this was an intentional act. The F.B.I.'s Baltimore office reiterated this sentiment, saying that there is no specific and credible information to suggest any ties to terrorism at this time."

The Congressman turned toward the Agent and said, "Does that phone have a secure line, and if so, may I use it?" The Agent nodded and handed Congressman Harris the telephone. "Could I have a short time in your office for a private phone call?" Said Mr. Harris, addressing the Agent. "Surely, Sir, take as long as needed, and I will remain outside until you finish your call." Was the reply.

The Congressman dialed the direct line to his office in Washington. The phone answered, and he asked his secretary, "What is the story of the bridge accident?" There was a short pause on the line before a reply was heard, "Sorry, Sir, I needed to move into the other office for privacy. My contacts at the C.I.A. tell me the ship was a cyber-attack from somewhere within the United States. They are unsure from where, but they are positive from within the U.S. The official word is that it was an accident or human error, but this was an attack. My contact mentioned that the attack had all the earmarkings of Chinese hackers written all over it. Does that help you, Sir?" The Congressman took a moment and replied, "Thank you, Bill, that will make today a lot easier for me," then he hung up the telephone.

Mr. Harris stood and exited, thanking the Agent on the way out for using his office. He returned to his chair and sat down to await the arrival of the guests. The Senior

Agent interrupted the wait with a request or an unusual question for the Congressman. "Sir, this entire thing is extraordinary, you know, detailing what the people arriving should expect or be entitled to. I think that the best person to deliver the message would be you. I know you cannot come to the island and provide this introduction every time guests arrive, but what if we tape the first one and replay it for all new guests? The message will be the same; frankly, we do not feel comfortable delivering such an important message." The Congressman momentarily thought about his answer, "I think that could be a great idea, and I will tailor the message to be more generic to accommodate future arrivals." The Congressman again sat back in his chair, cleared his head, and waited for the guests to arrive. As he sat patiently, he thought this could be the most important talk of his career. Mr. Harris was about to speak to people who disdain the law and didn't care about what anybody said. The Congressman thought this could be the highlight of his entire career. The Congressman bowed his head to ponder what he might say, interrupted by an Agent's voice from outside the building: "The plane has arrived. Prepare yourselves to meet the guest."

Chapter Eight

Welcome To Sanctuary

The Boeing 737 was directed to taxi to the west side of the runway opposite the large Navy hangar. The aircraft stood about seven hundred feet from the hangar at this location, well out of view from prying eyes. It is perfect for the guests to deplane, move into the small group bus, and transport into Sanctuary in groups of twenty.

Congressman Harris remained in the central office of the Border Patrol until Agents deplaned and transported all of the guests through the two large gates into The Republic of Sanctuary. Additional Agents received the guests at Building # 1 and moved them into Building # 2 after adjusting their restrains. Once the guests were seated and properly restrained in Building # 2, Congressman Harris walked the short distance through the gates and entered The Republic of Sanctuary.

Congressman Harris slowly walked past Building #1 and noticed a sign above the center door labeled 'Guest Receiving Area.' Looking through a window, he saw that it appeared to be a layout like a small bus station. Perfect, he thought to himself, just perfect. He smiled and continued his journey to Information Building # 2, where he hoped to define the meaning of The Republic of Sanctuary to the newly arrived guests. Entering by way of a rear entrance, he made his way into a sizeable auditorium area where over one hundred and twenty guests were waiting to find out why they were there. As he stood off the center of a small stage area, he could see many unhappy faces in the dimly lit room. Many sad faces wore translation headsets to convert English into their native language to avoid misunderstanding. He paused and felt like a comedian going on stage to tell an unwelcoming crowd of convicts jokes about being in jail. Taking a deep breath, Congressman Harris began the walk to the center of the small stage, stopped at the podium, turned, and looked into the faces of pure evil.

As he stood at the podium, he noticed the lighting above brighten slightly, and looking out above the guests, he could now make out the presence of three video cameras pointing directly at him to capture every movement and word. Placing the few notes he carried with him on the podium, he began speaking: "First of all, you have been handed a guidebook in the language of your choice giving details about The Republic of Sanctuary and its accommodations. I know you are all wondering where and why you are here. The Republic of Sanctuary is in the middle of the Pacific Ocean, approximately twelve hundred miles from the west coast of the United States." He could hear the low voices from the guests rumble, "What are you kidding?" Mr. Harris continues, "The Republic of Sanctuary has agreed to accept all persons being deported from the United States when the country of their origin refuses to repatriate them. You fall into that category today and are now residents and citizens of The Republic of Sanctuary." A guest attempted to stand in the back of the room, screaming, "I want to speak to my lawyer," but his restraints held him down. Congressman Harris scans down his list of guests to find to whom he was about to speak before replying, "Ah, Mr. well, I do not want to say your name here. First of all, I see that you are from Haiti; you entered the United States in 2023 and have been arrested seven times for molesting underage children. I am trying to find the word, oh yes, pedophile; that's what it says here, pedophile." Every eye in the large building was on the man from Haiti. Even hardened criminals hate people who prey on children, and this man from Haiti would be no exception.

Mr. Harris continues, "Sir, you are not in the United States, and I am unsure if the Republic has any lawyers. Based on the looks you received from your fellow guests, I believe that a lawyer may be the last thing you need."

The atmosphere in the room was now weighty from the last verbal exchange with the man from Haiti. Congressman Harris felt sure no one else would call out defiantly and risk exposing why they were here. He continued with the information he was there to relate, "I told you where and why you are here, and now I am going to tell you what here is all about. The Republic of Sanctuary is an island surrounded by special surveillance buoys. These buoys are approximately eight hundred feet from the shoreline and can detect unwanted movement. These buoys are the ocean border of the Republic. I must warn you, at this time, that these buoys contain laser-guided armaments that are accurate to within one inch at one hundred yards. Please do not attempt to approach these buoys, as they are ready and able to apply lethal force.

The large wall you enter through today is well-guarded with surveillance equipment. And, like the buoys, they are provided with lethal armaments. Stay away from the wall for your safety. You now know the limits of The Republic of Sanctuary. Now, let's speak about what is in the Republic itself.

The city is enormous, with ample housing for approximately two hundred thousand people. Almost all houses are identical in design, and only colors make them different. Every home has a telephone, but calls are limited to only the houses within the Republic. There is no access to the outside world from Sanctuary. Cell phone service is unavailable, and they will not work anywhere in Sanctuary." The information concerning the cell phones did not sit well, and several guests tried to get out of their respective chairs. The armed Border Patrol agents stationed around the room brought their arms to bear on the disruptive guests. Confronted with overwhelming force, the guests returned quietly to their seats, attempting to show their mean faces as they went.

Congressman Harris waited and continued, "A new A.I. system installed in each home will handle your medical needs, a system developed exclusively for Sanctuary. Medications will be delivered daily by the Border Patrol to the medical building in the city. The city center has a public library and laundromats throughout the city. Every home has a sixty-five-inch television and a catalog of over two thousand movies available through direct streaming from the control center on the border. The movies are constantly updated by border staff, available in several languages, and accessible twenty-four hours daily. The beaches along the island's western coast allow you to swim and relax. Boating is not allowed on the island, and again, you should not go anywhere near the buoys; it could be lethal."

Congressman Harris stopped, took a moment to sip a glass of water, and continued, "Sanctuary currently had two hundred electric cars parked alongside their houses, each with charging ports. The vehicles can only reach a speed of twenty-five miles per hour, and should a car come within two thousand feet of the border wall, it will shut down. There are six food stores in Sanctuary where you can purchase groceries for free. Each home has a cooking and dining area and all the other facilities one would expect to find in a home. The city has free places to shop for clothes and other necessities. The Republic of Sanctuary is a free place to live and enjoy your life. There is nothing to steal as everything is free of cost. The book you were handed by Border Patrol when you entered is full of details, so please read it."

Mr. Harris paused before speaking, "Oh, did I mention the laws of The Republic of Sanctuary? Well, there are none. You, the citizens, will define and enforce whatever laws you choose. If you like, you can make murder legal, and it is up to you to decide the rules and the penalty."

At that moment, Congressman Harris realized how afraid this group of thugs were. The guests' heads were all moving, and they looked around the room to see who would be there to help them if trouble arose. The vicious ban of people sitting before him used the laws of the United States to protect them while they preyed on the weak. Those laws were no longer there to afford protection, and now they needed to take care of themselves for the first time. They were all wolves and all sheep at the same time.

Congressman Harris finishes, "There are also warehouses with building supplies and tools to create new things. You will find some small powered equipment to move materials or build. Again, they will not function within the two thousand-foot barrier of the wall. You have a chance to change your lives and be productive, or you can continue wasting your time on this earth; it's your choice. Again, please read the book detailing how and when the Border Patrol will deliver supplies. The Border Patrol monitors and controls the power station at the island's southern end. Please don't go there and cause a power outage in your city. Your neighbors will probably not be happy sitting in the dark while the armed military repairs the station. This information session has ended." And the Congressman turned and left the stage.

As the Border Agents took the guests in groups into the city in the small bus, Congressman Harris walked back through the two gates, leaving Sanctuary. He thanked the Senior Agent for assistance and requested transportation to his waiting plane. The Senior Agent spoke, "Sir, I do have a question. One of the guests wanted to know when the women would arrive?" The Congressman smiled and said, "Oh, I forgot to tell them in there. This place is a male-only Republic." His transportation arrived, and he boarded and left the imaginary place called Sanctuary, heading back to Washington to continue the fight.

CHAPTER NINE

Returning Home

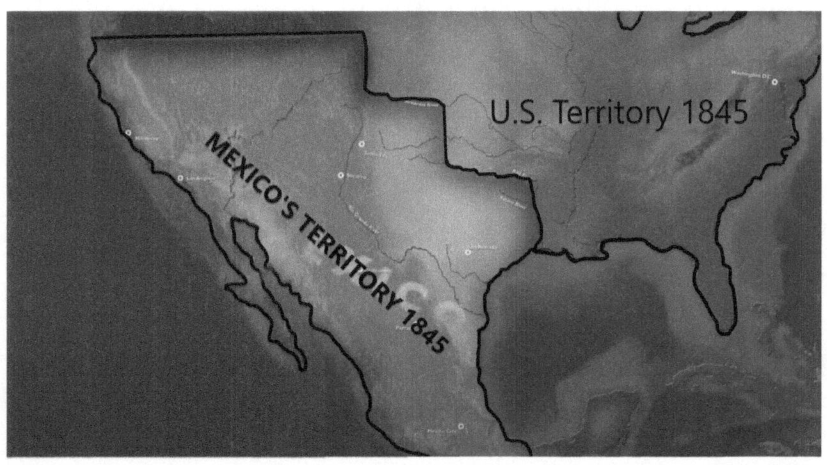

The Congressman's short flight back to the L.A.X. airport was brief and uneventful. As he walks to his departure gate, the demon thoughts pour through his head. Did he provide enough information for the guests today, and will the video work for the following guests? What did he forget to tell them? Is the video quality they made going to be good enough? There were so many unanswered questions that needed answering, so many questions. And probably none would be answered tonight.

Finally reaching the departure gate, he sat down and closed his eyes momentarily. His thoughts drifted to his wife and daughter and then back to the island. His mind acted like a ping-pong game back and forth between the things he loved and the things he hated. Being tired plays tricks on the mind, and tonight, he was exhausted. Anything decided tonight would likely be wrong, and he pushed the questions out of his mind. The Congressman had trained himself never to make an essential decision after three P.M. He believed decisions made after three in the afternoon were usually wrong, and tonight would be no exception. Any questions concerning today's events must wait until his head clears tomorrow morning when he returns home in good old Washington, D.C.

It was seven-thirty Pacific time when he boarded the plane to take him home to Washington. The direct flight should arrive around one A.M., leaving a half-hour car trip to his home and then directly to bed. Before taking his seat in first class, he grabbed a small pillow from the overhead storage. He thought this would come in handy to get some 'shut-eye' during the flight. As the large plane lifted off the L.A.X. runway, he sat back, closed his eyes, and drifted off to sleep in a mystical place where everyone loved each other.

About two hours into the flight, the Congressman was awakened by a voice over the airplane's intercom system. The voice belonged to the pilot, informing passengers that the aircraft was experiencing engine troubles and the plane was rerouting to O'Hare in Chicago for safety. The Congressman started a low but deep laugh as he sat almost motionless in his seat. A fellow passenger across from him inquired what was so funny as rerouting would delay them for hours. The Congressman looked at him, saying, "The airplane we are on isn't a Boeing; it's an Airbus. Thank God it's not a Boeing." Believing the Congressman had lost his mind, the fellow passenger inquired no further.

The flight ended safely at O'Hare airport, and the passengers were directed to gate twenty-eight to rebook a flight to Washington. The rebooking was quick and easy for a flight leaving at eight a.m. the following morning. The Congressman was handed his new ticket and turned to walk away, thinking, 'God, nobody, absolutely nobody, wants to go to Washington.'

Congressman Harris boarded a shuttle to a local hotel for the night to grab some sleep before departing to Washington in the morning, and Chicago became his home, at least for tonight.

After a short night's rest, he got up at six a.m. and headed to the airport to board the eight a.m. flight to Washington. Working through airport security, he wondered why even a Congressman needed to go through the mess. The airlines don't even trust a Congressman. Then he smiled. I shouldn't blame them. I work with these people, some of whom I can not trust to do anything right.

The hour-and-a-half flight to Washington allowed the Congressman time to review the questions from the day before. The main question or concern in his mind was the telephone call with his secretary, Bill, in the Washington office. Why would the C.I.A. believe the bridge collision was terrorism and not an accident? But that is what Bill said: Terrorist attack. What did the C.I.A. base that evaluation on? What information do they have that I do not have? What is a four-letter word that could speak volumes when the question of what actually happened is finally answered by the C.I.A.

Finally, back in Washington, the Congressman headed home to freshen up before going to the office. An hour later, he climbed into his car to travel to the Congressional Building twenty minutes away. Stalled in a traffic jam, Congressman Harris picked up his cell phone and dialed his office, "Bill, I am sitting in traffic about a mile from the office. Make a note that we should introduce legislation to fix these damn roads to relieve the congestion in the city." The voice on the other end of the phone replied, "Got it, Sir." And the call ended.

At one p.m., the front door to the Congressman's main office opened, and Congressman Harris stood in the door frame. "Good to have you back, Sir," his secretary proclaimed from behind his desk. The Congressman said, "I feel like a deadbeat coming in after one in the afternoon. I have so much to do and so many calls to make. I don't know where to start." Bill smiles and replies, "Start at the beginning, Sir, start at the beginning." The Congressman stops momentarily, then fires back, "The beginning is in my private office, and I need you there with me."

Laying down his briefcase, the Congressman drops into the leather chair behind his desk before speaking. "Bill, please sit down. Did your C.I.A. contact give you any more information about why they think the bridge collision was a terrorist act?" Bill raised his hand, shaking his head, and spoke, "No, he could not give me details as to why they think that, but he made it clear it was not an accident." Congressman Harris sits back in his chair before speaking, "Could I speak with your contact, even off the record, in a place that would not cause a problem for him or her?" Bill replies, "Sorry, Sir, the contacts I have made over the years will not meet with you and provide any information. Their superiors would end their career if they knew they spoke to me, let alone if they talked to a Congressman. But I am very sure, Sir, they stated it was terrorism and not an accident, and there was something about a signal transmitted over the Internet that took control of the guidance system just before the collision. A signal that originated from within the United States." The

Congressman lowered his head slightly to speak, "Well, who else could help fill in the blanks with this? Any ideas?" Bill leans forward to reply softly, "Well, there is a guy that the C.I.A. and Homeland Security use a lot for background information. Of all things, he is a history professor in the State of New York college system. I am trying to remember his name; let's see, maybe North or Norton, no, no, it's Norris. Professor Norris. My contacts told me he is a wealth of information, and Sir, you should be warned; he can create a conspiracy theory in a heartbeat. But again, the C.I.A. and others use him constantly for background. Maybe he can help fill in the blanks in this matter."

The Congressman leans forward to address Bill, "Find me this, Professor Norris, and arrange a meeting with him and myself. I don't know what he may be able to help with, but talk is cheap." "Yes, Sir," Bill replied, stood up, and left the office, given his task to find the elusive Professor Norris.

CHAPTER TEN
Enlightenment

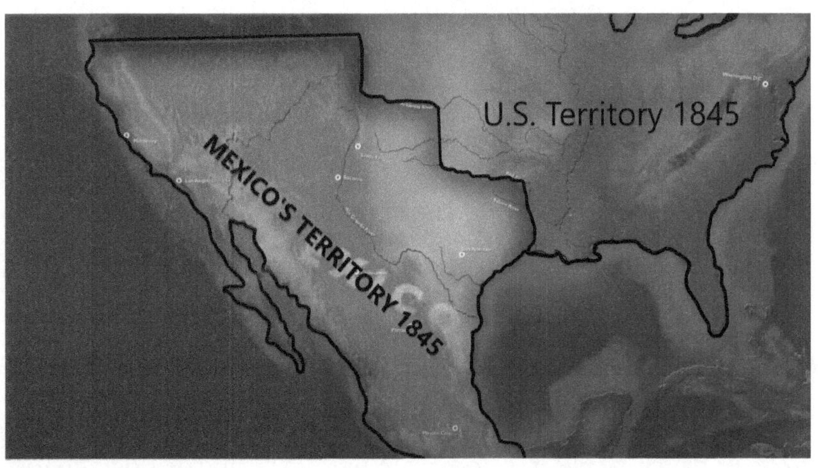

The meeting with Professor Norris was set for ten days later on a Saturday afternoon in Kingston, New York. Professor Norris set the time and place based on his leaving for a speaking engagement the following Monday morning, and he would not be available for almost a month. Congressman Harris agreed to this location and time and would make it a point to meet this infamous Professor Norris.

A small restaurant was the place, and noon was the time when the two sat down at a round table in the back room of the food establishment. Congressman Harris reaches the small table and speaks, "Professor Norris, I presume." The Professor, not liking to be upstaged, displays a big smile and answers only, "Yes." Not very much to hear from the man whom the Congressman hoped had the answers to all of his questions. After a brief pause, the Professor started, "And what do I owe the honor of your presence here today, Congressman?" Congressman Harris was still sizing up the Professor when the Professor finished. The voice did not fit a short, plump man of around sixty years of age. The voice was just too high a pitch for the Professor's body. Trying hard not to appear surprised by the Professor's voice, the Congressman began laying out the questions he hoped the Professor could answer. "Well, Professor, I understand through the grapevine that you are an expert on International affairs and world history." The Professor replies, "Apparently, you have never attended one of my lectures, or you would know the answer to that question."

"Well, no, I have never had the pleasure of hearing you speak," he replies. The Professor reached into a small bag he had brought and removed an entire folder of documents. "These will help you; you may find the future or fate of the United States in the documents within this folder." The Professor's voice was soft as he slid the folder across the table to the Congressman. The Professor continued, "Oh, by the way, who sent you to me, Homeland Security, C.I.A., or the F.B.I. who?" Congressman Harris took a moment before answering, "None of those agencies sent me to you. An old student of yours told me you were the man to see for answers, and here I am." "I am flattered." He replied. "But I thought someone from one of those agencies would have sent you. I see them sitting through my lectures and taking photos and notes. You can pick them right out of a crowd, and I refer to them as the perfect people. You know the type, not a hair out of place." The Congressman interrupted, "Excuse me, are you telling me federal security agencies attend your lectures? And if so, for what reason?" The Professor sat still and said, "Look in the folder, Congressman, look in the folder."

Congressman Harris opened the folder handed to him by the Professor. He found an index of topics on the first page. Two headings stood out as he scanned the page: Mexico retaking U.S. territory and China's efforts to disrupt U.S. shipping and trade. The Congressman looked from the papers, and almost as if on cue, the Professor echoed, "The bridge, Congressman, the bridge. It would be best to ask the right questions to find the correct answers. What are the Chinese known for today? Come on, think, Congressman, how about hacking the Internet and taking control of infrastructure? Balloons float across the country to evaluate from above the weakest parts of the U.S. trade, the ports. You can't sink a ship in the middle of a shipping lane without repercussions, but what if an accident occurred and a bridge collapsed and closed the port for years? Same result without an international issue. China could attempt to execute a plan like this from their soil, but it is too risky. The Feds could track the data traffic right back to China. However, if they had executed the plan from within the United States, it would have looked like a homegrown attack."

The Congressman stopped the Professor for a moment. He remembered what his Secretary Bill had told him, "according to his contact at the C.I.A., the attack had come from within the United States." He motioned for the Professor to continue. "Your next question should be, how did they get here? Well, the open border sounds about right to me. And your last question must be, where could they find a haven to work without being disturbed by the police? How about the Cartel safe houses within the United States? Congressman, the Chinese drugs are a deadly smoke screen to hide the actual mission. Don't get me wrong, they would love to kill a bunch of Americans for poisoning China with opium, but they want to bring the U.S. to its knees, and Mexico will offer to help the United States out by moving the illegals into the southwestern states, effectively giving them back control of that territory. Find the Chinese illegals that came across the border, and one of them will provide you with what you need to stop the invasion. Remember, the Chinese are very loyal, but their first loyalty is always to their family. Also, the shame of failure is unacceptable to the Chinese and considered worse than death. Use these against them, and someone will give you what you need."

Congressman Harris sat momentarily, trying to take in the Professor's words. Not speaking, he looked down at the papers spread out before him. Could Professor Norris have unraveled a plan to subdivide the United States and Mexico back into territories before the 1848 Cession? Conspiracy theory or fact? How would you go about proving something like this?

The Professor interrupted the Congressman's thoughts, "Sir, I need to pack to catch an early flight on Monday morning. Everything you need to solve this mystery is in the folder. Get the Chinese first, and the others will fall." The Professor slid back his chair, stood, and shook hands with the Congressman. As their hands shook, he repeated, The Chinese first." With that, the Professor turned and left the building.

Congressman Harris sat back down and waved to the bartender for service. The bartender approached the table with a warm, "What can I get for you tonight, Sir?" The Congressman smiled at the bartender and said, "I want the strongest drink you have at the bar, and make it a double."

The Congressman's home would be a Kingston, New York hotel room that night. Somewhere quiet where he could read and digest the craziest story he had ever heard. Mexico is taking back a large part of the United States, and China is destroying the infrastructure to help. He laughed at how silly the whole thing sounded but could not stop reading the documents before him detailing the plan. A plan that, if true, lay dormant for over one hundred and seventy-five years waiting for the right time.

Congressman Harris slept late at the Kingston, New York, hotel that Sunday morning. His head was still spinning with the information in the documents Professor Norris gave him the day before. Time is what he needed to think and rethink regarding the information the Professor had handed him. He had arrived in Kingston by train and had a return ticket to Washington but decided to rent a car for the return trip. Sometimes, a long drive gives new clarity to issues, and the documents in the folder need a lot of clarity.

After a quick checkout and a short shuttle bus ride to the car rental office, he was in a new Genesis GV80 seat. Sitting behind the wheel of this mid-size S.U.V., he adjusted the seat and mirrors and pointed the car toward the Interstate that would take him home. Whatever it is, there is something about a brand-new vehicle that makes you feel good about yourself. Maybe it is the new car smell or how tight and solid it feels. Whatever it is, it feels great to be on the road in a new luxury S.U.V. like the GV80 cruising the highways of America.

It is well known the Interstate highways covering the United States can be lonely places to travel. Your only companion is the tire noise as you glide over the paved roads and the wind as it caresses the sides of the car. Leaving the car's radio off creates the perfect place to think, dream, and make decisions. The noise of travel is soothing, and the mind can wander many paths, seeking the right solution to problems or reliving lost memories. Today, the Congressman's problems were tucked away in his briefcase, sitting on the passenger's seat. He first would fill his long five-and-a-half-hour drive home with his family's sweet memories. Memories of better times adrift through his mind's virtual time and space.

The adage, 'Youth is wasted on the young,' could not be truer, and it filled the Congressman's head as he adjusted the temperature and stared down the long highway on his trip back home. His memories shifted to when his brother and he were target-practicing with snowballs striking cars as the cars drove past. The Congressman smiled, and as he looked back, those were the good old days of fun where no one got hurt, and the most dangerous weapon was a snowball.

While he drove and enjoyed his childhood memory, he glimpsed at the briefcase on the passenger seat. He could almost hear it crying out what about me? All right, what about you, he thought. He lifted his cell phone and dialed his secretary at home. The phone rang five times without an answer, followed by a prompt to leave a message. The Congressman starts, "Bill, I hate to call you on a Sunday, but I am heading back to Washington, and I need you to do something for me on Monday morning. I was hoping you could find a way for me to meet with the Intelligence Committee no later than Tuesday of this week. I don't care who you must speak with, but I must make it happen. And I am sorry to interrupt your weekend. Goodbye."

The long drive continued while the images of the Professor's documents in the briefcase flashed through his head. There are so many questions and so few, if any, answers. The Intelligence Committee was his only shot at verifying the documents and developing a defense strategy if they proved true and correct.

CHAPTER ELEVEN

A Friend in Need

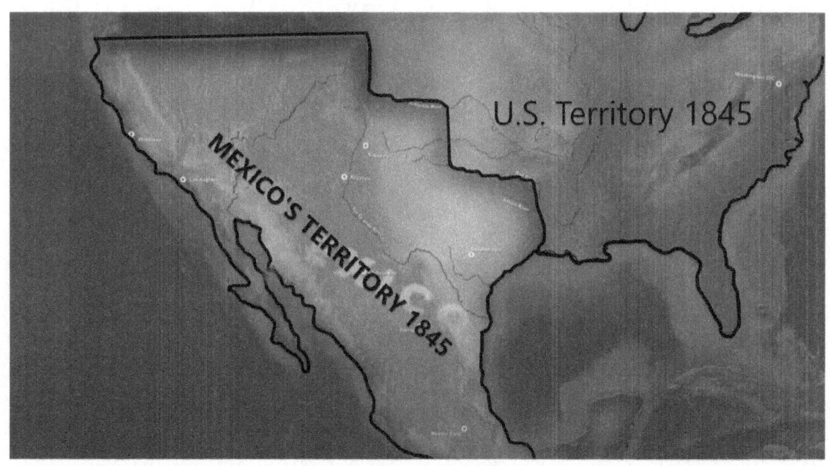

Congressman Harris found himself entering the Congressional building early on Tuesday morning. As he requested, his secretary succeeded in getting him before the Committee on Intelligence, and he carried a copy of the documents Professor Norris had given him over the weekend in his briefcase. He had two questions concerning the documents: first, are they trustworthy and correct, and second, could the Professor's theory of Mexico wanting back the territory they ceded to the United States in 1848 be true? The questions looked easy to answer on paper, but Congressman Harris had been in Washington for many years, and there were no 'yes' or 'no' answers in Washington.

He paused to compose himself as he reached the door of Chairman Tucker's office. He turned the doorknob and walked through the heavy wooden door. The office was slightly larger than his, and the furniture was of much higher quality. Papers piled deep alongside the computer monitor, leaving little room to work on the desk, a clear display of a busy man.

Congressman's Office

Standing near the door as he entered, he found Congressman Tucker reaching out his hand as he entered, speaking, "Good morning, Congressman; your secretary said you had something important to bring to the committee." Mr. Harris stopped before speaking, "Well, Sir, I believe I have something, but first, let me thank you for seeing me on such brief notice." "Anytime, Congressman," Came the reply. Chairman Tucker spoke next, "I think the best thing to do is for me to see what you have and then decide if it should go before the entire committee. I think that makes the most sense. What exactly do you have?" Mr. Harris opened his briefcase and removed the copies of the documents Professor Norris had given him. "Here is what I have for you to look at," stated Mr. Harris as he handed the documents to Chairman Tucker. He continued his assessment of what they seemed to contain, "According to this, Professor Norris believes that Mexico will try to take back the territory it ceded to the United States in 1848. This story sounds unbelievable, but the documents support at least part of his theory."

The Chairman pulled the documents toward him and began to read what they contained. Slowly turning the pages and making faces as he read. Finally, after several minutes, he spoke, "The documents seem to be credible as far as historical events, but I am having trouble linking as to how Mexico would get the United States to say, here it is, take it back. What leverage would force the U.S. to yield to such a request?" Congressman Harris replies, "Well, when I spoke with the Professor, he claimed that Mexico would use mass migration to force the United States' hand. The Professor also indicated to me that the Chinese would use their hackers to infiltrate the U.S., take down our infrastructure, and increase the pressure by using terrorists within the country to disrupt. According to the Professor, the drugs and trafficking are just cash for the Cartels, and it allows an overrun at the border to distract the agents, allowing the terrorists and hackers to get in without a background check. These are the people working with Mexico to force the return of the land."

The Chairman sat back and folded his hands before replying, "Let's say that everything in these papers is true. Without more solid proof of some real conspiracy against the country, our colleagues would laugh us out of the chamber. I can hear them now: Area 51, Roswell, the Kennedy assassination, and now Mexico forcing us to surrender several states back to them. I can't see China calling me and saying, 'Hey, our hackers are on the way to destroy your stuff,' or Mexico asking us to hand over California, Colorado, and Texas. With something like this, I would need a real smoking gun, and I mean absolute."

Congressman Harris takes a moment and says, "What about the bridge just destroyed by that container ship? What about that?" Chairman Tucker sits forward and leans on his desk before replying, "The official response is it was accidental and not an act of terrorism. Do you have any proof that someone intentionally caused it to happen? If you do, who and what is the proof?" Mr. Harris speaks slowly, "I have heard that some of our security agencies believe it to be intentional and not an accident." The Chairman stops him right there. "Congressman, I hear things all the time. I heard that China manufactured

Covid-19 in a Chinese lab. Then, I listened to the virus move from animals to humans. Then maybe it was just a natural thing of nature. I need someone to go before the committee and state under oath, 'I saw this happen, and I have other witnesses that will back up my story.' Hopefully, one witness will be a Democrat and the other a Republican. Congressman Harris, you bring me that, and I will have these documents and those witnesses before my committee the next day. Without that level of proof, these documents will go nowhere."

Congressman Harris replies, "Thank you for your time and honest opinion concerning these documents. If I get anything else, I will contact you." The Chairman and the Congressman both stood and shook hands to say good-bye. "Oh, by the way," The Chairman starts, "a great job with your other committee." Congressman Harris looked back as if puzzled, "What committee would that be, Mr. Chairman?" Chairman Tucker smiled before answering, "I heard the world has a new Republic as of a few weeks ago. I can't prove that, but I have heard that. Have a good day, Congressman Harris."

As Congressman Harris left the room, he thought about how secrets in Washington found themselves printed on the front pages of newspapers. He expected the next call he would receive would be from the President, either thanking him for a great job or telling him to report to the nearest gallows for public hanging.

He decided to walk back to his office several blocks away and review the meeting events. He summed up the meeting as documents look and maybe credible but go nowhere without anything else to back them up. Great, now where would someone go to find that smoking gun? Maybe advertise in a local paper that 'wanted one smoking gun to prove international conspiracy.' The other option, of course, is to wait and see.

CHAPTER TWELVE
The Report

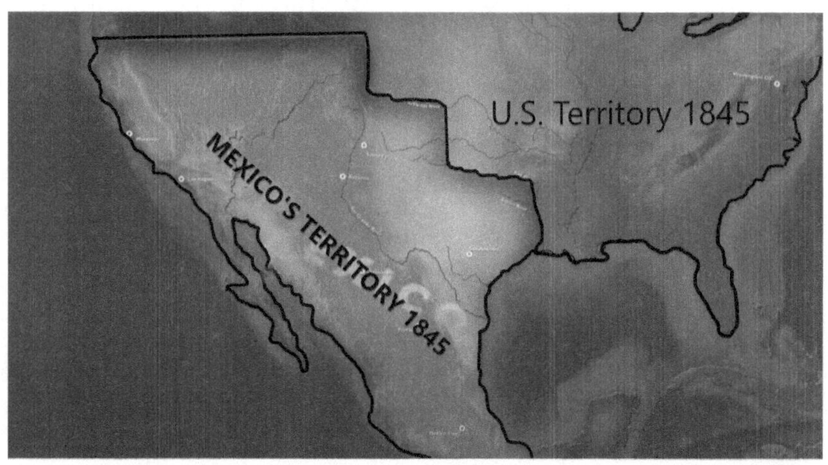

Eight weeks later, Congressman Harris received his first report from the Border Agents on the Republic of Sanctuary wall. The report detailed daily activities and logged issues encountered. Under the heading 'high priority issues,' he found the details of three bodies recovered.

The report read: "Over the last four weeks, Border Agents recovered and removed three deceased citizens of Sanctuary. The bodies were all left near the drop-off area of the central warehouse for food supplies so we could find them easily. Each of the deceased was transported and buried in the public cemetery at the southernmost tip of The Republic and given a proper burial on the day of recovery."

The Congressman looked toward the office ceiling and thought, 'My God, they are starting to kill each other.' His eyes found his way back to the report in his hand, and he continued reading. "Of particular note is the three people killed were all the head gang leaders in a large city. Agent found this a surprise because these three decease were possibly the most violent citizens in The Republic of Sanctuary."

The Congressman stopped reading again to review what this meant. Three of the most violent illegals removed from the United States are found dead near the area used to restock the warehouse. Whoever killed them wanted them found. Maybe it is a warning to others in the Republic? But why are there three and not twenty others? You would think the weakest in the Republic would fall prey to the most violent. He picked up a pen and circled the paragraphs he just finished reading. This information meant something and could not be discarded as chance killings.

The following paragraph of the report totaled the number of arrivals in the Republic by the week since he was last there. A quick look at the numbers showed over twenty-five hundred guests have arrived in less than three months since the first arrivals. It appears the black ice agents are doing their job of getting these violent people out of the States.

The next page detailed the food, material supplies, and fuel delivered to the Republic under foreign aid. A footnote detailed how Border Agents calculated the amount of each commodity needed by the number of citizens in the Republic. Inventory completed at the time of delivery showed the calculations to be correct, and agents will repeat them once per month.

The third page of the report caught the Congressman's attention with the heading, "Encounters and Escapes.' As of this writing, there have been no escapes from the Republic of Sanctuary. We have experienced two encounters along the divider wall, and a warning repelled the intruders. There was one challenge for the security buoys; the report follows: A person unknown attempted to swim between buoy numbers one-thirty-five and one-thirty-six at 2:00 am Wednesday. The buoy scanning cameras pick up the person's heat signature, and the buoy laser locked on the individual floating on a board at the one-hundred-and-sixty-foot mark. At the one-hundred-foot mark, each buoy shined a sighting laser on the individual, and a warning was sounded in three languages, telling the person the buoys were about to fire. Buoy number one-thirty-five fired a single twenty-caliber warning shot ahead of the intruder, and the individual turned around and left the buoy protection area, disengaging the buoy alert system. Note: The video taken by the buoy security cameras shows many citizens watching the encounter from the beach.'

The Congressman sat back in his deep chair with a smile, thinking, 'They must have thought the buoys were a bluff. And then his thoughts turned to the fact that a twenty-caliber gun is the same used on fighter jets to shoot down aircraft. I wonder how fast this person believed he could paddle that board?'

The Senior Border Agent signed the report detailing the Republic of Sanctuary and dated it.

The Congressman sat back in his chair with a feeling of some relief. Looking around his office, he thought the report could have read three hundred bodies recovered instead of three. But why were all three leaders of gangs in a big city? Three leaders must mean something to someone, but who? I can call a psychiatrist and ask the question. How should I start, "Well, sir, we found three dead bodies of leading gang members from big cities; what does that mean?" I can not tell the Doctor anything about the Republic of Sanctuary. I can not tell the Doctor how they discovered the bodies. I can not tell the Doctor anything other than three dead bodies discovered somewhere at some time. With that limited information,

I am afraid the only thing the psychiatrist could answer is they are indeed dead. He may even request I come to his office for testing, as the whole thing sounds crazy. The only person who may be able to help would be Professor Norris. I could present this as a theory based on history, and maybe he can give me insight into what happens when outside forces push people together on an island.

The Congressman pushed the button on the intercom, summoning his secretary. A click followed: "Yes, Sir, what can I do for you?" Answered the secretary. "I need to speak with Professor Norris again. Can you please contact him and let me know when he is available? Tell him I will even buy him dinner." The Congressman concluded.

The Congressman returned to re-read the report, ensuring he missed nothing significant in his first reading. The only thing that kept sticking out was the three gang leaders found dead. He knew it must have a meaning, and he hoped Professor Norris could explain why those three died and not three hundred.

The Congressman's answer concerning Professor Norris came over the intercom at three p.m. that same day. "Sorry, sir. The best the Professor can do is three weeks from this Friday." Said the secretary. The Congressman replied, "Thank you. Let the Professor know that will work for me, and make reservations at a nice restaurant where we can have dinner. Someplace quiet, if possible, would be great." That said, he lifted the intercom button and returned to his computer to work.

CHAPTER THIRTEEN

The Gang of Three

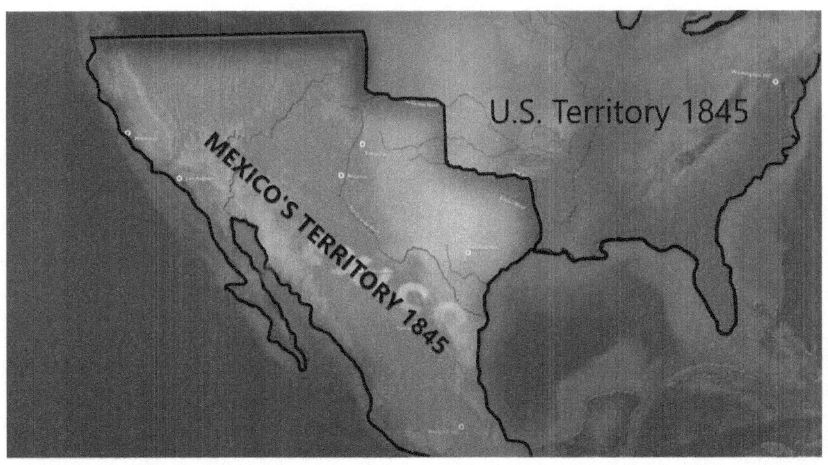

It was nine a.m. when the first limousine arrived at the ranch in northern Mexico, just five miles from the U.S. border. The building was a single-story adobe-style home with a dome-covered entryway. Like the last meeting location, El Mencho selected this place because of its isolation away from prying eyes.

Adobe House Meeting Place

The security guards at the ranch arrived before sunrise to occupy their positions encircling the entire ranch. El Mencho exited the first limo and walked across the lawn area and directly into the house with his two bodyguards. Minutes later, a second Limousine arrived carrying the President of Mexico and the Ambassador of China. Like El Mencho, they exited the vehicle and walked over the lawn and into the house, followed by several armed guards and a Chinese interpreter. One of the armed guards stopped under the dome-covered front door and would remain throughout the meeting.

They were struck by the ample open space inside the main living area as they walked through the ranch's large front door. Once inside, a young woman directed them into a small side room where El Mencho was waiting. Once seated, the meeting began with El Mencho addressing the parties. "Thank you for coming here today on such short notice. I called you today to discuss what we need to proceed with our plan. I am sure you have noticed that most of our friends in this endeavor are not here today. I have intentionally not invited them today so we can iron out issues. First, I have a problem with the two Haitians from the last meeting. They never spoke about completing the mission, only how much money they would get from it. I don't feel we can trust them; they must be watched. I think they would rat us out in a heartbeat." El Mencho paused momentarily to see his guest's reaction before continuing. "Our good friends who represent the Islamic states. Five of their people have been arrested in demonstrations, waving flags and yelling death to America. I sit and watch them on television, drawing attention to themselves. I sent a message to their leaders who attended the last meeting voicing concern about the actions of their people. I will repeat today the answer I got back as it is too unbelievable. They messaged me back," 'We understand your concern, but you must also understand our people have been oppressed for years by the other faiths, and sometimes they react out of their love and praise for Allah. We will advise them of your concerns, but it is unlikely to alter what they do to honor our God. I hope you understand our position in this matter.' El Mencho finishes reading the message and pauses, waiting for a response. All three in attendance looked at one another for a moment in disbelief of what the message contained. The Ambassador spoke through his interpreter, "A total lack of discipline without the ability to control oneself. They will bring trouble, and the group should remove them."

El Mencho nodded before saying, "And let us not forget Iran. Instead of laying low and waiting for the correct time to take revenge, they openly attack Israel directly from Iran." El Mencho paused again to see his guest's reaction. Lifting a glass of water to his lips, he allows the guest time to speak. Neither the President of Mexico nor the Ambassador said a word. El Mencho began again, "I have learned our good friends in South America have been trying to cut special financial deals to accept the return of their citizens from the U.S. Our agreed plan was to over-load the U.S. with illegals and refuse to take them back. "We planned to move as a single entity against the United States. Everyone at the meeting agreed to a coordinated effort to complete the mission. We three seem to be the only ones willing to execute a plan without each of our people going off doing whatever they want."

The three men sat quietly for several moments before the President of Mexico spoke, "Our goal has always been to retake the territory stolen from us by the Americans. That has not and will not change. I am disturbed to hear our South American friends have been trying to make secret deals with the U.S. for money. We and the group of South American countries agreed we would negotiate all deals to keep the U.S. off balance. I am disappointed but not surprised by hearing this. El Mencho, do you believe

we are at a point where we can overrun the South Western U.S. States with our people and force a surrender of
that territory back at this time?" El Mencho replies, "We
needed more time to move many more people across
the border. I will need to contact the other Cartels and
issue instructions on moving people from the northeastern part of the U.S. to the southwestern part. Our original plan was to move large numbers to the Northeastern cities, like New York and Chicago, to overload their
economy. Sooner or later, the federal government must
stop the collapse by borrowing money from worldwide
sources. At that point, China could raise interest rates,
further draining the U.S. even at a faster rate."

The Mexican President interrupts, "What is happening in California? I know you pushed a large number of
people into California when Texas blocked the border."
El Mencho again replies, "The politics in California are
favorable for overtaking the U.S. residents there. They
have already started to issue driver's licenses and allow
illegals to work. In time, the U.S. residents of California
will become dependent on the illegals. The big buck Grin-
gos think they are in control, but their lives will change
when they do not have anyone to work for them as we
control the illegal workers. People are fleeing California
in large numbers to other U.S. states. Soon, California will
have two classes of people: the wealthy and the poor.
The poor will control the state by sheer numbers, and

we will control the poor." "But El Mencho, how long will this take?" Replied the President. El Mencho shrugs his shoulders before answering, "I think it will take another two years to reach the tipping point."

The Mexican President leans back in his chair before speaking, "Do we have that long? The United States will have an election soon, and the administration may not be as favorable as it has been to leave the border open. Can we move the timetable up?" El Mencho, looking at the floor, says, "We must be careful and not expose our Cartel people in the U.S. to the police. Moving too fast leaves a lot of loose ends and mistakes. I will address this with the other Cartels and see if it is possible."

El Mencho turns to the Chinese Ambassador and says, "I saw on television news a bridge accident with a large container ship. A large U.S. port has been taken out of commission by some unknown force of nature. The news states it was an accident, and I am sure that is what happened. Do you agree, Ambassador? The Ambassador smiles before speaking, "I don't want to speculate about what happened to their bridge. Maybe it was just bad luck, or maybe some cosmic intervention. Not sure." El Mencho smiles back, "That is what I like about you and your people. I don't remember you ever showing your hand, even to your friends. But there are two things I need to know, one concerning the next shipment of the chemicals to make our drugs. When and how much should we be expecting? And two, how many hackers are in a position to shut down the U.S. infrastructure?"

The Ambassador leaned forward in his chair before answering, "The Chemicals you need are currently on a ship and will land in Puerto Libertad in three weeks. As for the amount, let's say it is the largest shipment to date. And for the second question, we already have inserted into the Chinese illegals twenty-four agents able to hack the United States Infrastructure. The number of Chinese we allowed to leave China and come to the United States exceeds five hundred. We felt this would be enough to hide the agents and defeat their true identity discovery should the group of Chinese be questioned."

El Mencho again took control of the conversation. "I believe we have concluded today as to where we stand. The Haitians can not be trusted. Mr. President, it would be best to regain control of the South American countries and get them in line. And, as far as Iran and the other terrorists, I don't think we should include them in anything. They are too unstable and will endanger the entire plan."

The attendees all stood and exited the room. Today's meeting at least gave them a firm foundation for where they stood. As they exited the home, the midday sun beat down on the earth around them as they passed through the front door and into the welcoming air conditioning of the limousine. And as before, a meeting that never happened concluded.

CHAPTER FOURTEEN

Professor Norris Comes Through

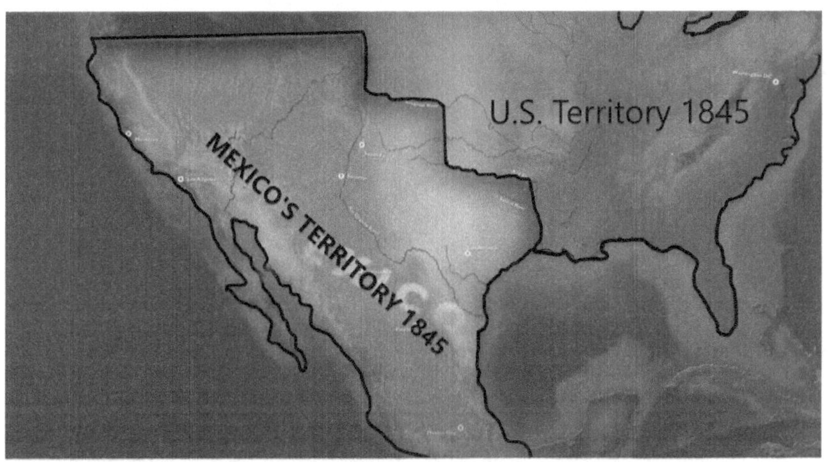

Congressman Harris arrived just before seven p.m. at the Torra Bar & Restaurant in Manhattan. The restaurant is located on the eastern side of Manhattan and advertises itself as a 'Little Italy' style eatery. The red brick front with two large windows invites passersby to come on in and enjoy some great Italian food. The aromas the Congressman smelled led him to believe the food might be great as he walked to the booth-style table. Still, tonight, he was there to discuss the information Professor Norris provided and the secret report from the Senior Border Agent. As the Congressman stood before the booth, he thought about how perfectly this would work out. The curved booth would allow the Professor to sit close enough to discuss the serious matters in the report privately without being overheard.

Curved Restaurant Booth at Torra Bar &
Restaurant

The Congressman sat on the right side of the booth and placed his briefcase on the seat toward the center. While he waited for the Professor, a waiter put a glass of water in front of him and asked if he needed anything while he waited for his party to arrive. The Congressman shook his head left and right to indicate nothing was required, and the waiter left the table.

About ten minutes passed before the first glimpse of the Professor occurred. Dressed in plaid slacks and a non-matching jacket, he perfectly fit the image of a Professor. The Congressman lifted and waved his left hand to signal his location to the Professor. The Professor acknowledged the wave and headed to where the Congressman was seated. As the Professor approached, the Congressman stood and extended his hand to greet the Professor by saying, "Good to see you again, Professor."

The Professor replies, "It is also good to see you, Congressman. To what do I owe the pleasure?" The Congressman gestures for them to take their seats and says, "Before we get down to business, let's order some of this great food." The Professor smiled and picked up the menu to order while the Congressman browsed down the long list of menu items. The waiter stood patiently waiting for their selections. Once the waiter left, the Congressman asked the long-awaited questions he had for the Professor to answer.

"Professor," He started, "I need a theoretical question answered. What are the possible results of placing a group of different gang members on an island without laws or restrictions? But, supply them with food, shelter, and all other needs." The Professor looked puzzled momentarily before answering, "Well, I guess you would have created a form of a penal colony. Australia was once a penal colony that eventually evolved into an independent country. Without laws and regulations, the residents would need to fend for themselves. Eventually, however, they would need to form their laws and methods to enforce them. Even bad people must find a way to live or co-exist together. If food is an issue, they may fight over the food supply. But if there is ample food supply, there is no need to fight over food. And the same would go for shelter and otherworldly needs." The Congressman stopped momentarily before speaking, "And if you were to find a few of the residents dead after a short time, what I mean by that is the leaders of gangs from different cities. What would that mean?" Professor Norris responds, "Damn, this is a detailed theoretical question. If the dead were all at one time a leader of a gang per se, it likely would mean the lesser gang members were tired of taking orders from a dictator and wanted a more equal society to live in. I would not be surprised if they took a vote to kill off the gang leaders. It could be the beginning of a democratic society they are forming from within. I can see where they would kill the tyrants to make everyone equal."

The Congressman sits back in the booth and says, "So you are telling me the residents of such a place could be moving toward a government and creating their laws?" Professor Norris leans forward before speaking, "I am telling you that dictators maintain control through threats and violence. The population must address the dictators before a law-binding society can exist."

Congressman Harris sat motionless momentarily, and his thoughts turned to Sanctuary. Could the Republic of Sanctuary eventually evolve into a law-abiding country? The Professor interrupted the Congressman's thoughts, "Congressman, Congressman, What other questions do you have?"

The Congressman, awakened from his dream, responds, "Oh, yes, Professor. I have been reading through the documents you gave me. You seem to infer that the Mexican Cartels are the driving engine for a takeover of the United States. And you also state that Mexico wants to take back all the territory lost in 1848 to the United States." The Professor butts in, "That is correct." "Well," The Congressman continues, "How exactly are they going to do that?"

The Professor breathes before speaking, "Let me start it from the beginning. The Cartels do not care about who occupies the land. They will make money, no matter who governs the land, the United States or Mexico. So, they do not care if Mexico controls whatever they control. Mexico wants it back because of a pride issue, as they are very proud. Mexico can not contact the United States and ask them to return it. The United States would laugh at them. But, if the territory is home to a large Mexican population, Mexico controls it. And should the United States find itself in financial problems with the world, there may be an opportunity to take it back." The Professor lifted a water glass and drank before continuing, "Well, what about China? Europe and the Western countries poisoned China for years with drugs. The countries acted as drug dealers, killing the Chinese people for many years. China wants to replace the United States as a world leader. To do that takes money, and drugs are a great source of money. The Chinese are into the drugs up to their eyeballs, and they sweet-talk the world into believing they are trying to stop the drug trade. Bull-shit! The Chinese don't care if fifty million Americans die from a drug overdose; after all, how many Chinese died when the West was the dealer? But the drugs are only part of the plan. China has the best computer hackers in the world. They have spent years studying our infrastructure systems and attended our colleges. The Chinese sold the United States cranes to unload ships they could hack into and shut down. The hackers are here, Congressman. The hackers are here. They came in with the large number of Chinese illegals and are hiding in plain sight. Round up the Chinese illegals, and you will find their hackers that are going to shut down the country: one last thing, Congressman. Did you ask how Mexico could overpower the United States? An old military story follows: 'The United States goes to war with India. Remember that India has a population of about one and a half billion people. On the first day of the war, the United States captured one million prisoners. On the second day of the war, the United States captured two million prisoners. On the third day, they capture three million prisoners. On the fourth day, India contacts the United States and asks if they will surrender yet. How many illegals have made their way into the United States? I expect a request from Mexico soon for the United States to surrender."

The Congressman sat staring into the space above the Professor. He looks down before speaking, "If I only had proof of what you are stating is fact. Anything I could point to and say, there it is." The Professor replied, "The bridge, Congressman, the bridge."

Then their dinners arrived, and the two men enjoyed a great Italian meal. The Professor and Congressman had gotten what they came for a good meal and information. When the meal had ended, they again shook hands and promised to keep in touch before leaving the restaurant.

As the Congressman hailed a cab, the only word that echoed through his mind was 'proof.' He had all the information and needed the 'proof' before anyone would believe this crazy story.

CHAPTER FIFTEEN
The Unwilling Informant

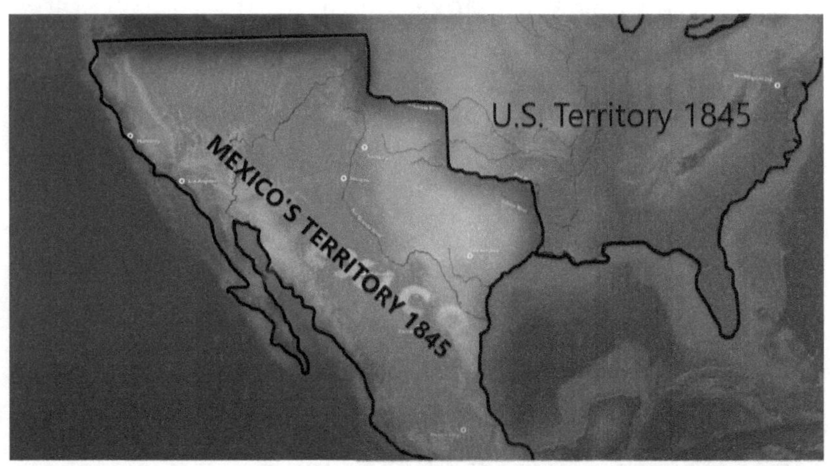

Renel Destina entered the room led by a Black Ice agent. Mr. Destina was still in handcuffs and chains from when Black Ice agents arrested him in Florida earlier in the day. Renel was pushed down into a wooden chair, overwhelmed by the three agents in the room. For minutes that seemed like hours, no one spoke a word, a stare down of good versus evil. Three agents sat on one side of the table, and Renel sat alone on the other.

The agent sitting in the center of the table spoke, "Well, Mr. Destina, it says here that you are the leader of the Grand Ravine gang in Haiti." Defiant Destina replies, "I don't know what that paper says, it might even be blank, and you are full of shit." The agent replies as he lifts and turns the document so Destina can see it. "It's not blank, Mr. Destina. It's a full report of who and what you are." The agent continues, "Mr. Destina, do you know a Jimmy Chérizier, AKA 'Barbecue'?" Destina lifts his head before replying, "I don't think I have ever heard of him. What's his name again?" The agent repeats, "Jimmy Chérizier, nickname Barbecue." "No, I don't think I know him," Destina replies. The agent smiles and then speaks, "That's funny he knows you. We got word that he was looking for you to talk with you about the money you stole before heading to Florida, where we picked you up earlier today." The agent paused before speaking, "Now, since you do not know him, I guess Mr. Destina, we are done here today." The prisoner leaned back in his chair with a big smile, taunting the agent.

The agents looked at each other before the agent on the left spoke, "Well, that settles it; I will personally put you on a plane back to Toussanint Louverture Airport in Port-au-Prince tonight." Destina jumped out of the chair, screaming, "You can't do that. I want asylum. I want to go to New York City. I have family and friends somewhere in New York. I have rights." The agent on the right chimes up, "Sit down, Sir. I do not think you understand Florida's laws. Florida is not a sanctuary state, and you were lawfully detained illegally entering the United States through Florida. You are now in our custody, and we have the sole decision regarding whether you stay. Since you do not know this 'Barbecue' person, you are not in danger, and we have decided to return you to Haiti." Destina, again on his feet, "You can't do this. He will kill me. Are you people stupid?" The agent replies, "You told us you do not know him, so why would someone you do not know want to hurt you? You will be on a plane back to Haiti tonight. And to be sure you will have no problems returning, I will let them know you are on the way." Destina looked at the three agents individually and said, "I have something to trade. Something big. But I want protection. They will all be after me. I want protection."

The three agents sat back and waited for more information to flow from Destina. The center agent spoke, "Well, what do you have for us, and how can we be sure it's not bullshit. You already lied about knowing 'Barbecue,' so why should we trust you?" Destina lowered his head before speaking, "I was there at the meeting in Mexico when they laid out the plans to take back the land and attack the United States." "Who is going to do what?" The agent questioned. Destina answers, "What do you mean who? Come on, man, Mexico, China, the Chinese hackers, and the terrorists, that's who."

The center agent slowly stood as he spoke, "Sit there, Mr. Destina. I need to get someone else involved in what you are about to tell us." The agent left the room and traveled down the hall to his office. Sitting at his desk, he lifted the phone and dialed a number to call his superiors in Washington. As the telephone answered, he said, "Congressman Harris, I need you in the Miami office. We have a guy here from Haiti who is claiming he was at a meeting in Mexico to take back land from the United States, and he also mentioned something about Chinese hackers and terrorist attacks. You should come here, Sir; it may be important." The Congressman responded within seconds, "I can grab a military flight to Miami and be there tonight. Keep this guy away from everyone. I don't want anyone speaking with him until I get there. Is that understood?" "Yes, Sir." The agent responded and hung up the phone.

The Congressman called out to his secretary in the outer office, "I need a military flight to Miami today. No excuses. I need to be in Miami as soon as possible." As the Congressman gathered up papers from his desk, he verified that he still had the folder he had received from Professor Norris. Opening the folder, he thumbed through to page seven. The professor highlighted, "Chinese Hackers are the key to the attacks." This person may be the break the committee was waiting for. No one outside a small group of congressmen and agents knew about Chinese Hackers. Where did this guy hear about it? And if he knows about the hackers, what else does he know?

The Air Force plane carrying Congressman Harris arrived in Miami, Florida, at six-thirty p.m. that evening. Air Force security transported the Congressman to F .D.C. Miami, a Federal prison about forty-five minutes from the Miami International Airport. F.D.C. Miami was where the Black Ice group of Florida was detaining Renel Destina. Mr. Destina claimed he had information about Chinese hackers. Congressman Harris remembered Professor Norris's warning about Chinese hackers, who he believed were involved in an attack on a bridge in Baltimore that occurred weeks ago.

As expected, Warden Shields of F.D.C. Miami was still waiting for the Congressman to arrive, and he informed the Congressman that all prison facilities and staff were at his disposal. The Congressman requested that they retreat to the Warden's office to discuss what would be needed for the interview with Mr. Destina. The Congressman began the conversation with, "Mr. Shields, thank you for waiting for me to arrive. I don't have much time, so I will get directly to what I need to interview Mr. Destina. I will need an interview room with video-taping capability. The Black Ice officers who performed the initial interview should be there. And your highest ranking officer here tonight to sit in on the interview as an outside witness.

How long will it take to put this together?" The Warden replied without hesitation, "I can have this room and the staff you requested ready in one hour. Will that be acceptable, Sir?" "That will be good, Warden. One additional thing: I want bottled water, soda, and hot coffee on the table in the room. We don't need reasons to leave the room during the interview. Lastly, is there somewhere I can freshen up before the interview?" The Warden stood and pointed to his right, "This way, Congressman, you can use my private facilities; I hope they are satisfactory." The Congressman walked through the door, shutting it behind him."

One hour later, a knock on the door signaled to the Congressman that everything was ready for the interview. The Congressman picked up the briefcase containing the documents from Professor Norris and exited the room. He was taken down a long windowless hallway to a room marked 'I7.' The door opened, and inside, he found the three Black Ice Agents and a senior prison staff member waiting. The four men watched closely as the Congressman entered the room, sizing him up, one would say. After a few steps into the room, he stopped and spoke, "I am Congressman Harris, and I am sure you know why I am here tonight. I don't need to tell you how important this interview could be, so I will not waste your time. I will ask the questions. Please agree with whatever I say to Mr. Destina." Looking back toward the door, the

Congressman says, "Please have the prison staff escort Mr. Destina in."

A tall prison staff member led Mr. Destina in handcuffs and chains and placed him in a chair. Once he was seated, the others in the room sat facing Mr. Destina. Congressman Harris began the conversation, "Mr. Destina, I am Congressman Harris. I understand you have something you want to tell me. Is that correct, Mr. Destina?" The Congressman stopped and waited for his answer. Mr. Destina scanned the faces of each person present before answering, "That depends upon the deal you have for me." The Congressman sat back in his chair before replying, "Here is how it works in my world, Mr. Destina. You have illegally entered the United States of America. You are in the custody of Federal Agents, who are by law supposed to deport you back from where you came. You do not wish to return because you claim someone will hurt you. Have I got it right so far, Mr. Destina?" Destina nodded in agreement, and the Congressman continued, "At first, you denied knowing this person called 'Barbecue.' Then a miracle happened. When the agents informed you, they would return you to Haiti. You told them Barbecue was going to hurt you. So, let us clear this up right here and now. Do you know this Barbecue person?" Destina nodded his head. "Is he going to do you harm, Mr. Destina?" Asked the Congressman. Destina nodded again.

The Congressman opened his briefcase and removed a small pile of papers before speaking, "Mr. Destina, you told these agents something about a meeting, and you have information concerning said meeting for help from us. Is that correct?" Destina looked down and replied, "Yeah, I was at a meeting." The Congressman waited for more, but nothing followed. "Well, Mr. Destina. What was the meeting about, where was the meeting, and who was at the meeting?" The Congressman asked. "What's the deal first?" Replied Destina. The Congressman picked up his papers and exclaimed, "You have nothing for us, Mr. Destina." Turning to the agent on his right, he says, "How quickly can you get this guy back to Haiti?" The agent looks at his watch before replying, "Next flight to Haiti is in about an hour, Sir." Destina stood up from his chair, yelling, "You can't send me back there. Barbecue is waiting for me, and he is going to kill me. I can't go back there!"

The Congressman sat back down while an agent pushed Destina into his chair. Congressman Harris paused and let Destina collect his thoughts about his situation before speaking, "Mr. Destina, If you have the information I believe you have, I will personally guarantee your safety and likely placement into a witness protection program. If you sit here tonight and give me any more bull shit, your ass will be on a plane to Haiti tonight. Do you understand me, Sir?" Destina looked directly into the

Congressman's eye and saw he was serious about this threat.

With fear in his eyes, Destina started the story of the meeting as the agents and Congressman took notes. "Our Mexican Cartel contacts told Barbecue and I about a meeting in Mexico near the U.S. border a few months ago. We conned our way into the meeting by telling the people running it we have people already in the U.S. who could help in their efforts to disrupt the police using our gang members." The Congressman interjected, "Who attended this meeting?" Destina paused before speaking, "There was this guy El Mencho, some big shot Cartel head. And maybe four or five other Cartel heads at the table. Oh, and the President of Mexico was there, as was an ambassador from China. Down on our end of the table sat someone from the country of Iran, and he was surrounded by people who claimed to belong to terrorist groups such as ISIS-K or something like that. Oh, yeah, the guy from Iran was some special guard head. I think the others referred to him as a Publican guard. There were also others to translate Spanish into other languages, and these Middle Eastern guys spoke all different languages."

Congressman Harris interrupted the conversation, asking, "What was this meeting about? I mean, what were they thinking about or planning? Destina replies, "Hey man, first of all, Barbecue and I were only after money. We did not want to kill people or destroy a bunch of shit, just money, nothing else. These other dudes from the Middle East are into killing all Americans. That was what they were there for: to kill as many Americans as possible. The head guy, El Mencho, seemed to be in control of the whole thing, and he kept boasting about how many of these control rooms the Cartels had set up in the United States and how all the illegals were under the control of the Cartels.

The Ambassador from China kept assuring El Mencho that China had shipped large amounts of drugs, and they were on the way for the Cartels to sell in the United States." The Congressman interrupts again, "You said the President of Mexico was there seated at the table? How do you know he was the President of Mexico?" Destina answered, "El Mencho introduced him as the President of Mexico at the beginning of the meeting. Yeah, the President of Mexico told us he was not running the meeting as he wanted something called 'plausible denial' if someone found out about the meeting. I don't understand what that means, but he said that. Oh, I almost forgot; several other people from South American countries representing their countries were there. They never spoke at the meeting; they just listened."

Congressman Harris took a moment and whispered something to the agent sitting on his left side. The agent stood and left the room without speaking.

The Congressman turned back towards Mr. Destina and opened the pile of documents on the table before asking the next question. "Did the President of Mexico say why he was there at the meeting?" Destina started to laugh before answering, "He said Mexico was going to take back all the land the United States stole from Mexico over a hundred years ago by flooding the U.S. with illegals." Congressman Harris paused and then asked, "You said something to the agents about 'hackers' before I arrived. What did you mean by that?" Destina shrugged his shoulders while speaking, "I don't know a lot about that kind of shit, but the Chinese guy said they were able to get over twenty of these hackers buried into the Chinese illegals with the help of the Cartels. He talked to El Mencho about how they were going to use the Cartel's control rooms to break all the United States shit and take the U.S. to its knees. I think he said. If I remember it was part of Mexico taking back the land because the U.S. could not afford to pay for the illegals and keep the United States running. My take on the meeting was that they were all going to work together to screw the United States. Again, Barbecue and I only wanted the money not to kill anybody."

After speaking with Congressman Harris, the agent who had left the room returned with photos of different people. The Congressman took the pictures and passed them across the table to Destina. The Congressman looked at

Mr. Destina and said, "Please look at these pictures and see if you can identify them and where you can place them. Put the ones you can place on your right and the others on your left." The pile of pictures consisted of approximately one hundred different people. Destina slowly looked at each photo, moving most of them to the left and a few to his right. While they waited, the Congressman and other agents sipped the beverages the Warden supplied without speaking or showing expression. When Destina finished looking through the pictures, the Congressman picked up the pile on Mr. Destina's right.

The Congressman stood and said, "Mr. Destina, I am going to ask you who you think each one of these persons in the photo is and where you know them from or have seen them. Can you do that?" Destina replied by nodding his head. As the Congressman slid the first photo across the table to Mr. Destina, he spoke, "Who do you believe this person is?" Looking up from the photo, Destina said, "That's the Publican guard guy from Iran." "And this person, Mr. Destina, who is he?" Destina replies, "That's the President of Mexico, but at the meeting, he was not wearing a suit, just everyday clothes." What about this person? Asked the Congressman, "That's the Chinese man, the only one wearing a suit at the meeting." And this one said the Congressman, "That's El Mencho, but at the meeting, his hair and beard were different."

Although there were remaining pictures Mr. Destina had identified, the Congressman decided to stop the interview. Congressman Harris stood up from the table and said, "I think that is all for tonight. Mr. Destina, you will remain in the protective custody of these agents until I can work out something to keep you safe. I highly recommend you tell no one about being here tonight and what we have discussed."

The interview for that night was over, and the Congressman requested an official flight back to Washington. He finally had the smoking gun he needed to proceed, and time was of the essence. As he waited for transportation to take him back to the airport, he spoke with Black Ice agent Murray. "What do you think, Sir?" Murray asked. The Congressman paused before saying, "Agent Murray, I could explain how he identified the President of Mexico or maybe even El Mencho from the news or something he saw reported in the past. But, he could not have seen this picture of this man anywhere but at a meeting he attended. This picture is classified and from Israeli intelligence. The Israelis and the United States have been trying to find this guy for almost four years. He is the head of the Revolutionary Guard and is a coordinator of terrorism around the world. What would he be doing in Mexico if Mr. Destina's story is not true?"

Congressman Harris was unaware at the time that El Mencho had called it correctly: don't trust the Haitians.

CHAPTER SIXTEEN

The Intelligence Committee

Congressman Harris arrived home around three a.m. after the interview with Renel Destina in Miami, Florida. His mind was still racing over what they had learned from the interview, and the Congressman climbed straight into bed without showering. Awakened by the all too familiar alarm clock at seven-thirty, he slowly rolled over and placed his feet on the floor one at a time. He could not miss work today as he needed to be in the office as early as possible to transfer the vital information he gathered to the Intelligence Committee.

Arriving at his office building just after nine-twenty, he walked directly to his office. As the Congressman opened the door, his secretary greeted him, "Good morning, Sir. I hope your trip to Florida bore fruit." The Congressman replied, "Not only fruit, Bill, I think I have the entire tree to work with. Could you arrange an immediate pick up by Secure Courier Service? I need something delivered today to Congressman Tucker, Chairman of the Committee on Intelligence, as soon as possible." Bill replied, "Yes, Sir, I will have them come over immediately and pick up whatever you need to send to Congressman Tucker. Will there be anything else you need me to do this morning, Congressman?" Congressman Harris stops in the door frame of his office and turns before speaking, "Yeah, get Congressman Tucker on the telephone so I can tell him to expect a package." With that said, the Congressman passed through the door, closing it behind him.

The office intercom buzzed moments later, and Bill, his secretary, announced Congressman Tucker was on the secure telephone line. The Congressman answers the phone, "Good morning, Chairman Tucker. I am sending you a videotape of an interview I held last night in Miami. Please watch it immediately. I believe national security is at risk, and the information is on the tape. You asked for a smoking gun. Well, here it is. Buckle up, Mr. Chairman.

Your Committee may be in for a rough ride. Call me back after you watch the tape. Goodbye." And Congressman Harris hung up the phone.

Congressman Harris handed the courier a package containing a copy of the taped interview. The courier slid the package into a secure pouch, locked it, took down the delivery information, and left his office en route to deliver it to Chairman Tucker. Congressman Harris decided to go out and get a good cup of coffee to help kill time until he heard back from Chairman Tucker concerning the tape.

Almost two hours had passed before the telephone in Congressman Harris' office rang. As he picked up the phone, a voice on the other end said, "Harris, this is Tucker. Please come to my office now. I will convene the Committee as soon as you arrive." Followed by a click as Congressman Tucker hung up the phone.

Congressman Harris had barely entered the building when security escorted him into a Sensitive Compartmented Information Facility, often called a 'SCIF.' After a few minutes, all the members of the Intelligence Committee walked into the room for the briefing. Congressman Tucker played the taped interview of Mr. Destina without interruption as the Committee looked on. When the tape finished, Congressman Tucker addressed the other members of the Committee. With his head down, he speaks in a low voice, "For too long, we have sat in a room like this trying to convince ourselves that the illegal migration into the United States was benign and going to work itself out. I have no reason to believe that everything Mr. Destina stated during that interview is untrue. I have attached a photo of the head of the Revolutionary Guard from Iran to the papers in front of each of you. This photo comes from Israeli intelligence and is not public. This person's image has never appeared anywhere other than in the files of Israeli intelligence. Yet, Mr. Destina picked him out of almost one hundred pictures placed before him and called him the 'Publican Guard' guy. Mr. Destina claims this man attended a meeting in Mexico months ago to plot against the United States. Mr. Destina also named and identified several other high-ranking foreign government officials at that meeting, including the President of Mexico. They are trying to execute the plan using the documents I placed before you. We in this room are both Democrats and Republicans. I do not want to hear bickering between you about how this can or can't happen. The most persuasive information from Mr. Destina concerns Chinese hackers. The meeting occurred before the Baltimore Bridge accident. As of today, I have received word from intelligence that someone took control of the navigation system just before the ship crashed into the bridge. I was also informed the transmission that altered the navigation system came from within the United States. I can not point a finger at anyone and state that's the guy who did it, but the most likely suspect is the

Chinese. Congressman Harris has been working behind the scenes for some time addressing similar issues. It is alleged by some he formed a new republic called Sanctuary. Some also allege that a Black Ice group acts alongside the Federal I.C.E. to deport illegals from sanctuary states and cities. I need a vote to increase the number of the alleged Black Ice group members and fund it under the 'Black Ops' program."

Every Congressman raised his hand to support additional funding for more Black Ice agents.

Congressman Tucker continued, "I checked with Border Patrol before this meeting to see if there was a question on the entry paperwork for race or nationality. Specifically, is there a box to check if the person came from China? Border Patrol informed me there is such a box on the form. They also informed me that the Border Patrol gave every undocumented person a cell phone so they could be tracked. Congressman Harris, I am requesting you take the lead on a unique project to identify and locate all undocumented people who originated from China. You will need many more Black Ice agents, and the Black Ops funds to support this effort will be available by tomorrow. Harris, find these hackers and make sure they can do no further harm to the country. Congressman, please leave the documents I provided on the table before you. We do not know of any Black Ice group in existence or how it is funded. After Congressman Harris gains control of this problem, we will decide how to handle the diplomatic side of the issue."

Congressman Tucker stands and says, "This meeting is now over." The meeting room was now empty, leaving only Congressman Harris still sitting and trying to grasp what had just happened. His thoughts turned to his wife and daughter and the good times of their lives. Although there were many, the good times were about to be over-shadowed by the most challenging task of his career.

CHAPTER SEVENTEEN

The Search Begins

The meeting with the Intelligence Committee the day before was still vivid in Congressman Harris's mind. One word summed up the task he was given, 'How.' How do you find Chinese hackers who entered illegally and dispersed throughout the United States? How do you identify a Chinese hacker from other Chinese illegals? How do you detain Chinese illegals long enough to do background investigations into who they are? That damn three-letter word, how, keeps getting in the way of a sound answer.

He sat back deep in his chair behind his office desk and closed his eyes. This task can't be as difficult as creating an entire country, and we have accomplished that. It was then he realized the word he was looking for. The missing word was 'we,' as in the secret committee that approved The Republic of Sanctuary.

Pressing the intercom button alerted the Congressman's secretary he needed assistance. "Yes, Sir," came the response over the intercom. "Bill," the Congressman began, "I will give you a list of congresspeople I need to meet with later today. Contact them and tell them we must perform a special task again. They will understand. See if we can schedule this at my house around seven p.m. tonight. Also, Bill, I have some research for you this afternoon concerning available federal facilities. And Bill, this is important, so get it done." A click over the intercom ended the conversation.

The ride home was exceptionally long that day. To once again ask these dedicated people to work behind the scenes and likely outside the law made the Congressman feel uneasy. If anything should go wrong, the Intelligence Committee made clear they would deny any knowledge of the Congressman's actions. But he had no choice but to request assistance as this task was too large for one man.

He arrived home ten minutes before the scheduled meeting and hurried into the house to prepare to greet his guests. As always, the committee of Congressmen arrived precisely at seven, stood on the porch, pressed the doorbell, and waited for the door to open. Congressman Harris opened the door and extended his right hand to greet his guest. The Congressman repeated as each member walked by, "Good to see you again, and the dining room is at the end of the hall." A minute later, the Congressman joined his guests in the dining room.

"Please take a seat." Said the Congressman, and he waited for his guests to be seated. Congressman Harris addressed his guest at the end of the long table. "The last time we were in this room was to celebrate our success in creating a new republic. And that success continues today and into the future. You, the good people here, made that happen. Tonight, I am asking you to join me in another adventure. This one will be as rewarding as the first if we can do it." Everyone at the table sat up straight in their chair. The Congressman continues, "As always, we will be on our own, and no agency will be willing to help should we get into trouble."

The Congressman paused momentarily and then continued, "Our mission, should you accept it, is to find every Chinese national that came in illegally, detain them, debrief them, do a background check on each, and determine if they are a hacker. I know you thought I would give you something tough to accomplish, but this is all we need to do." Everyone at the table began to laugh.

Congressman Rudin, seated on the right side of the long table, raised his hand to be acknowledged. "Sir, what would be the driving force behind putting us on a task like this? Could you tell us what is behind this and, better yet, how we will make this happen?" Congressman Harris, in his most confident voice, speaks, "The Baltimore Bridge incident was not an accident but caused by Chinese terrorists. We have information from sources in the Intelligence agencies that Chinese hackers came into the United States embedded in groups of illegals. From our information, they intend to disrupt or destroy the United States infrastructure. That is the reason behind the request for us to take action. Next, how could we do it? I checked with border patrol and found that every undocumented person entering the United States fills out a set of forms. Each undocumented person must fill in a place on the forms for race or nationality. That means we can identify the Chinese that came into the United States."

Congressman Rudin, seated on the right side of the long table, again raised his hand to be acknowledged. "What about the Chinese that did not come through the border patrol agents, the 'gotaways?' Congressman Harris replied, "I thought about that, and my take on it is knowing the Chinese, they would not take a chance of getting caught sneaking into the country. Why when they can walk right in, fill out a form, and go anywhere in the country? Why risk getting caught and deported? So, my best guess is most, if not all, walked in and filled out the forms. Also, the undocumented Chinese were all given cell phones, yet another way to trace them." Congressman Harris paused, checking for more questions.

The secret committee sat silently, waiting for more information. Mr. Harris continues, "So I believe we can locate most Chinese that came into the country. We need to screen them by age first if the person is sixteen or younger, likely not a trained hacker. Suppose the person is forty-five or older, likely not a trained hacker. So we can narrow people down by age group to shrink the number of possibilities. I have been informed by border patrol that the total number of Chinese who enter is around five hundred and fifty. That is important as fifteen million people have entered the country in the last three years. Before I came here tonight, my secretary went through available federal facilities in Florida and found one suitable for our needs. Homeland Security has already agreed to make this facility available to process detainees to verify their background."

Congressman Cohen, sitting three seats down on the left, responded. "Sounds to me like you have a lot of this thing planned out, so why do you need us? And I've listened to you keep stating we will pick them up;

who exactly will pick them up?" Congressman Harris replies, "Thank you for that, Congressman; the Intelligence Agency has authorized me to hire five hundred additional Black Ice agents for this mission. That is the who will pick them up part of the question. The part about why I need you to help is simple. There will be a great deal of oversight of staffing and facilities with this project. I can not be everywhere and do it all. I need people I can count on and trust to get this done. The safety and well-being of the United States may well rest with us in this room. Please give me a show of hands if you are willing to do what is needed." Congressman Harris stood and watched as every hand raised in support in the room. He looked to his left before speaking, "Thank you for trusting me. I will continue to work details out and be back with you within the next few days."

The evening meeting ended as the Congressman, one by one, exited the dining room, walked down the long hall, and passed through the door onto the street.

Congressman Harris locked the front door, climbed the stairway to the bedroom, and went to bed, knowing he had just created another non-existent committee.

CHAPTER EIGHTEEN

The Chinese Connection

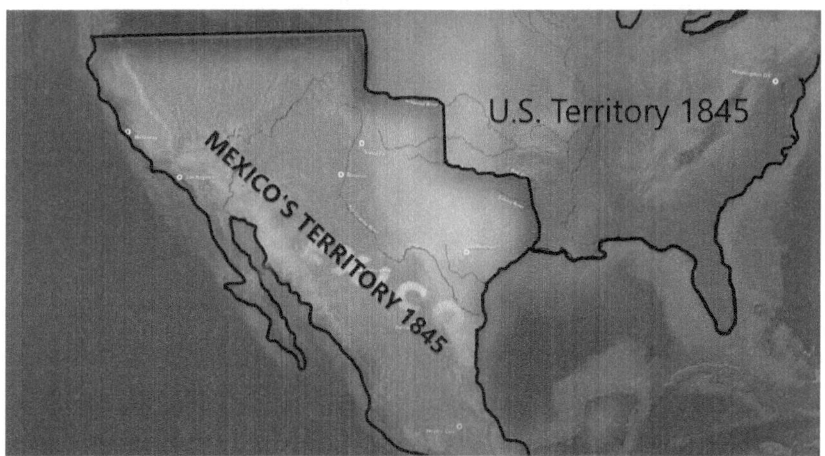

Congressman Harris sat in his office checking the calendar on the wall for the correct date. The calendar indicated a week had passed since the meeting at his home, where he formed the special committee to locate and detain the Chinese hackers living in the United States.

During this time, Congressman Rudin traveled to Florida and spent the week preparing the newly acquired

Federal Florida facility for detainees. Congressman Rudin reported back the facility needed some repairs but would be ready to receive detainees in ten to fourteen days.

Congressman Smith was assigned to work with the Black Ice group commander to hire new Black Ice Agents to work directly on the Chinese hacker project. Yesterday, he messaged Congressman Harris, saying they had hired over two hundred already trained agents.

Due to a labor shortage at the Border Patrol head-quarters, Congressman Moore and Williams were sifting through Border Patrol records at a Texas field office for forms marked as Chinese nationals. Luck was on their side when an administrative officer informed them that temporary employees had scanned most undocumented forms into a mainframe computer. A senior Border Patrol officer issued them a login and password, and the two congressmen had access to over ten million undocumented forms electronically. They advised Congressman Harris they would have the names and possible locations of all or most of the illegals marked as Chinese in two days.

The remaining three congressmen worked with the Black Ops finance staff to obtain the funds needed for the project. The Black Ops staff advised the congress members that taking over a federal facility required gentle handling to avoid detection by auditors that could blow the cover of Black Ops.

Congressman Harris had remained in Washington to coordinate the project from one central location. Still, tomorrow, he needed to return to Miami to re-interview Renel Destina, the informant from Haiti. Harris sat in his office wondering how and when the Black Ice agents would find its first Chinese hacker. He remembered what Professor Norris had said about the Chinese; they would rather die than lose their honor and use it against them. Before I can use anything against anyone, we need to find them. He turned to his computer and began reading the long list of e-mails he had not answered. My God, he thought, there was so much to accomplish and so little time. The only people with time were the hackers, as they had all the time in the world.

Ten a.m. the following morning, Congressman Harris was on a southbound plane to Miami. His destination was F.D.C. Miami, a Federal Detention Center, to meet with Renel Destina, the unwilling informant. As the plane touched down in Miami, F.D.C. Miami staff was waiting to transport the Congressman to the detention facility. The Congressman slid into the rear seat of a large Ford S.U.V. without speaking and, twenty minutes later, arrived at the facility. As the S.U.V. pulled up to the facility's front entrance, the Congressman slowly exited the vehicle, reaching back in to grab his briefcase. Turning away from the car, he walked to the large glass-enclosed entrance. Upon entering the building, the Congressman was confronted by a large metal detector blocking entry. As he began to place his belongings into a basket, he heard a voice echoing in the distance proclaiming, "Sir, no need to go through there," a door off to the right opened, allowing passage. The Warden stood on the other side of the door, hand extended, saying, "Good to see you again, Sir. I hope you had a good trip down from Washington." The Congressman replies, "The trip was perfect. How is my friend Mr. Destina doing?"

As the Warden and Congressman made their way to the Warden's office, he briefed the Congressman on Mr. Destina's living conditions. "Mr. Destina is receiving excellent care here at my facility." Said the Warden. "We are feeding him food from the staff kitchen, and he has been allowed to use the exercise area without restriction." The Congressman says, "I want to be sure he is kept in good spirits as I will need him in Washington in the coming weeks before a committee." "I understand, Sir." Answers the Warden.

They reached the Warden's office, where the Warden unlocked the thick wooden door. The Warden pushed open the door, and the two men entered the room. The Congressman noticed the room seemed neater or more organized since the last time he was there. It was apparent someone decided to make the office appear more professional. Laying his briefcase on a chair, the Congressman begins, "Warden, I will need the same room as before. Everything must be videotaped and recorded. I will also need one of your senior staff members as a witness and beverages in the room." The Warden replies, "Congressman, I have had everything arranged, and I will have Mr. Destina moved into the room at your pleasure." The Congressman walks toward the Warden's private bathroom, saying, "Give me ten minutes, and I will be in the interview room and ready to start." The Congressman enters the bathroom and closes the door.

Mr. Destina and the Senior staff member were seated when the Congressman entered the interview room. And as per regulations, a guard stood by the door as a deterrent for trouble. The Congressman wasted no time and started the conversation, "Mr. Destina, I understand you have been treated fairly here at this facility." Mr. Destina, nodding his head, replies, "Not bad, I only wish there was take-out or delivery here." The Congressman looks to the Senior staff member and asks, "Can Mr. Destina receive a food delivery here at this facility?" The Senior staff member replies, "I will look into that, sir."

The Congressman opens his briefcase, removes some documents, and says, "Mr. Destina, we believe you have been accommodating, and as I promised, I would work toward securing your safety. I have talked with the Federal Prosecutor in Florida, and he believes you may be eligible for the witness protection program offered by the Federal Government. I must clarify that you may lose your protection if you contact any of your relatives while in the program. Also, if you violate any laws, you can and will be deported back to Haiti. Do you understand what I just told you, Mr. Destina?" Destina nodded his head, showing he understood. The Congressman continues, "We may need you to testify before a Congressional committee at some point; is that also agreed upon?" Destina nods his head again in acceptance.

Congressman Harris slides a paper over to Mr. Destina to sign. Mr. Destina signs the paper and pushes it back across the table to the Congressman. "Now that is out of the way, let me tell you why I am here today. Today," Began the Congressman, "I need you to tell me anything you saw at the meeting in Mexico that appeared out of place or unusual. Did anything strike you as odd?" Destina looks down before replying, "Well, seeing high-ranking government officials sitting with Cartels and gang mem- bers seemed strange." The Congressman repeats, "Any- thing else that seemed strange?" Destina pauses before answering, "One of the guys with the Ambassador from China. He never spoke while at the table, but during a break for lunch, he was constantly on a laptop computer in a corner. Not that being on a computer is strange, but while on the computer, he appeared to be reading from a kid's book at the same time. He would read a little from the book and then type on the computer." The Congress- man interrupts, "How do you know it was a kid's book?"

Destina replies, "Because I walked over and picked it up to look at the bright-colored pictures of a dragons and other creatures. This guy got mad and grabbed the book back from me. I only wanted to see the bright images. I couldn't read the damn thing it was in Chinese. It just made me feel disrespected, that's all."

The Congressman leans back, "Are you sure it was a kid's book, Mr. Destina, and not something else?" Destina looks directly at the Congressman, "I could see several pages in the book, and they were pictures of dragons and other serpents in bright colors. There was not a lot of writing, just pictures. It was a kid's book." "And how old was this person, Mr. Destina, the one reading the book?" Asked the Congressman. Destina looks down to his right, "About thirty or thirty-two maybe, definitely not in his twenties." Congressman Harris repeats, "Was there any-thing else about the place you were at or someone else at the meeting with something distinctive about them?" Destina shook his head and said, "Nothing I can think of stands out now. I'm sorry."

The Congressman stood from his chair, "Mr. Destina, I will have you transported to Washington to appear be-fore an Intelligence Committee in the next few weeks. After that, the Florida U.S. Attorney will arrange for your witness protection. If you think of anything else that can help me, I gave the Warden my card with a direct telephone number. Stay out of trouble, Mr. Destina, as this deal is a once-in-a-lifetime deal. Don't blow it."

Congressman Harris left the room with his briefcase in hand. On his way back to the Warden's office, he kept thinking about Destina's claim of the guy reading a kid's book while typing on his computer. Damn, he thought, that does seem strange, but maybe the guy had a limited attention span or something, and the book helped it. Whatever it was, it made no sense, at least to him. Reaching the Warden's office, he requested a ride back to the airport to Washington. His flight was still over three hours away, but something about the soothing noise of an airport allowed him to place his thoughts into a logical order. Besides, who would want to sit around a prison?

CHAPTER NINETEEN

We Are the Dragons

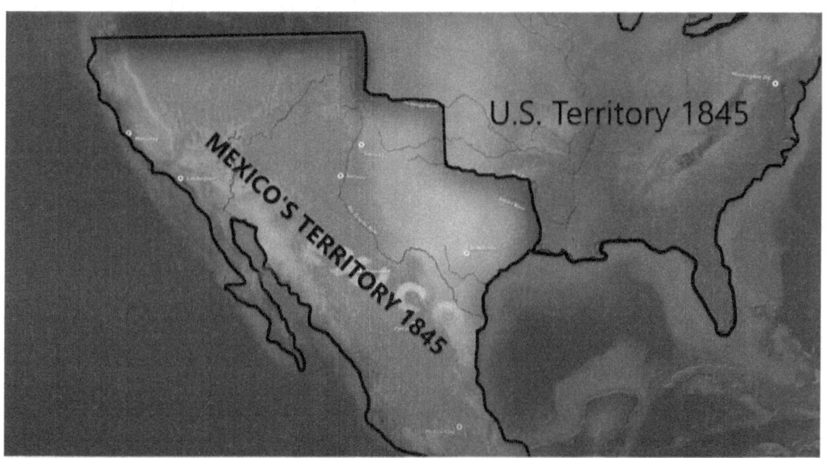

T ime, time is the devil of all things. Cars will age and rust in time. Roof shingles will dry and begin to leak in time. And Chinese saboteurs will prepare and strike in time. The clock was running, and time was the one thing that Congressman Harris did not have to waste.

It had been over a week since he left F.D.C. Miami, where he interviewed Renel Destina. Destina was not the perfect witness to anything, and when others asked questions concerning Mr. Destina, the Congressman referred to him as his reluctant informant. But reluctant or not, Destina was all he had, pointing to a Chinese connection.

Congressman Moore and Williams submitted a list of possible Chinese hackers three days ago. The list contained over two hundred people who could fit the criteria of a hacker. The list was limited to persons over sixteen years old and younger than forty-one. However, finding over two hundred people somewhere in the United States will still be no easy task. Congressman Harris turned the list over to the Black Ice group shortly after receiving it and was waiting for a report on anyone on the list being located by the group.

The phone rang as Congressman Harris sat in his office reading his e-mails. A quick "Hello" found Congressman Rudin on the other end of the line. "We're ready in Florida, Sir, and the facility is ready to receive detainees as we speak," echoed the voice over the phone. Congressman Rudin continued, "Tell Black Ice we are ready and waiting for them. As they say on that game show, 'Come on down.'" Congressman Harris leaned back in his chair before answering, "Great job, Congressman. You were the last part we needed to put this thing into motion. Take the rest of the week off. On second thought, stay there until I see where Black Ice is in their process. I'll call you back within the hour." And the Congressman hung up the telephone.

The Congressman presses the button on the intercom and then speaks, "Bill, that special phone number I gave you last week. Could you get that person on my private line for me? Thank you." The secretary did not reply, and a minute later, the private phone in the Congressman's office rang. The Congressman lifted the telephone and spoke, "Hello, Harris here." "Agent Williams, Sir," was the reply. The Congressman asks, "How is the Fishing going? Williams responds, "Fishing has been going well, Sir. Seven are in the bag, and another is hooked and waiting to be reeled in." "That is great," the Congressman replies, "The cannery is ready in Florida to receive the fish. When can they be delivered so I may inspect the catch?" Agent Williams takes a moment before replying, "Well, Sir, it is late afternoon here. We can transport them in the morning and have them there by four p.m. tomorrow. You will probably be able to start interviews the following day." The Congressman paused before speaking, "I will be there in two days to start interviews. By the way, some of your agents will need to staff the Florida facility. Bring them with you, and I will arrange a more permanent staff after my visit. When you hooked these fish, did you gather up their personal belongings? And if you did, make sure it all gets transported with them to Florida. One more thing, Williams, by any chance, did anyone have a kid's book about Dragons in their possession?" Agent Williams pauses and replies, "We took everything they had into custody, and I believe two of them had a Dragon Kids book." Harris replies, "Could you tell me the name of the book agent, Williams?" The Congressman could hear papers moving in the background over the phone. And then Williams speaks, "Let me see here, where is the name? Oh, Yes, here it is. 'We are the Dragons' is the title of the book. But that's not going to help, Sir. They are written entirely in Chinese other than the title." Congressman Harris responds, "Williams, isolate those books from their property and ensure they get delivered to me in Florida." Williams responds, "I will take care of everything, Sir, goodbye." The telephone call ended as quickly as it began.

Congressman Harris turns to his computer and starts to type. 'Google.com, We are the Dragons.' The screen displays the front cover of a book with a large, bright-colored Dragon for sale on Amazon. Damn, the Congressman thought Destina was right again. There the book is. A mouse click took the Congressman to Amazon and displayed the book, 'We Are the Dragons.' The Congressman reads the ad, 'Available in Kindle for download for $2.99 or Hard Cover for $42.99. Available in Chinese only.' He whispers to himself, "Inflation is out of control. Forty dollars more to get the printed version." Well, he thought, I guess the government can afford to spend the two dollars ninety-nine cents for a download copy and he ordered the book. A minute later, he opened the downloaded copy of 'We Are the Dragons' on his computer. The book looked like Destina described it, with bright-colored Dragons and Serpents on each page, followed by writing, all in Chinese. I wonder if this book is popular in China for some reason. Maybe it depicts a celebration of something, or it is cultural in some way. The Congressman sits back in his chair, leans over to his desk, and presses the intercom button for his secretary. "Bill, I know this is going to sound stupid, but I need you to call Amazon and find out something about a book for me." Bill replied, "A book, Sir?" The Congressman stops him, "Yes, Bill, a book. Tell them who you are and take as long as needed, but I need to know how long it has been on the market and how many of the books have been sold. Tell them I will vote for something they need the next time legislation comes up to help them." A simple echo of "Yes, Sir" came over the intercom. "And Bill, one more thing. I would like to know this today if possible. I don't care if you need to speak with the C.E.O. himself to get it." The Congressman released the button, and the intercom went silent.

The Congressman returned to his computer and started the page-by-page review of the book he purchased, wondering, 'Why would a Chinese person in a crucial meeting be reading a kid's book and working on a laptop?

The pictures were highly detailed animations, but what could they contain besides the Chinese text below?

The Congressman again picked up his telephone, dialed the F.B.I. field office in Washington, D.C., and waited for the phone to be answered. "This is Congressman Harris," he started, "Do you have anyone in your office or nearby that can read Chinese?" The person who answered the phone was caught off guard, "Well, Sir, ah, give me a moment, and I will have that answer for you. Please hold." The telephone went silent for almost a minute when a second voice answered, "Sir, Agent Wilhelm, what can I do for you?" The Congressman repeated, "Do you have anyone in your office or nearby who can read Chinese?" Agent Wilhelm responds, "We have an agent specializing in Asian and other Chinese dialects here at our office. I am sure he can assist you. Is this an important matter, or can it wait?"

The Congressman takes a moment before responding, "I would not be calling you, Sir, if it were not an important matter. I am a sitting Congressman and not a pollster." The reply was swift, "I will get Agent Zhōu immediately, Sir." And the Agent placed the telephone on hold again. The next voice answered, "Agent Zhōu, what can I do for you?" The Congressman, still aggravated with the first agent, spoke directly, "I need you to read a book I can send to your office. It appears to be a children's book, but I am unsure as I cannot read it. Please check it out today and tell me what it is. It will be in the secure F.B.I. drop box in five minutes. The title is 'We Are the Dragons.' I am sure you have my direct number, but I need to know what this book is today." Agent Zhōu only replies, "Yes, Sir." And the telephone disconnected.

Congressman Harris prepares the book to send to the F.B.I. drop box, still aggravated with the first agent and thinking, 'I wonder if Vladimir Putin called over to the K. G.B. main office if they would ask him if it was important?' Then, the Congressman presses the send button on his computer, transmitting the book to the drop box.

The Congressman stood and walked to the door leading out of his office. Opening the door, the Congressman noticed his secretary's chair was empty. He checked his watch and realized it was five minutes after twelve, which meant lunchtime. Well, nothing will happen for a while now, he thought. I might as well go out and get some lunch like the rest of the world. The Congressman grabs a jacket from the closet and ventures into the Washington D.C. world in search of something to eat.

A short lunch led to a long wait before Bill, his secretary, knocked and entered his office with the information he requested about the book. "I have it right here, Sir." Bill started. "The book 'We Are the Dragons' has sold forty-nine copies. It was published six months ago by a Chinese business owner. The breakdown of sales is twenty-five downloads and twenty-four hardcover, and there is no paperback version. No royalties have ever been paid to anyone, as the account on file is invalid." The Congressman turns his head and thanks Bill for the information. The door closed as Bill left, and the Congressman began to make notes on his computer. The notes read, "Forty-nine sold total. Twenty-five electronic downloads and twenty-four hardcover." He noted that someone had purchased twenty-four of each type if I bought one electronic download. He found it odd that the same number of books were purchased electronically and in hardcover. Also, why would someone pay forty dollars more for a book of pictures they can download?

Picking up the telephone, he dialed the F.B.I. Washington Field office and asked to speak with Agent Zhōu. Agent Zhōu picked up the phone, and the Congressman began, "Well, did you have a chance to read 'We Are the Dragons?' Agent Zhōu responds, "Yes, Sir, I did take time to review the book." The Congressman interjects, "Well, what do you think about the book?" Agent Zhōu replies again, "The book is a sort of children's book by all appearances. Strangely, it is written in two different Chinese Dialects. I can not relate it to any Chinese celebration or anything like that. Frankly, the book is poorly written at best, and I would be surprised if it sold a single copy." The Congressman interrupts, "So you saw nothing in the book that seems strange to you or would alert you to some other reason for the existence of the book?" "In my opinion, Sir, it is a poorly written children's book with overrated pictures of Dragons and Serpents." Agent Zhōu replied. "Thank you for your time, Agent Zhōu, and have a good day." And the Congressman hung up the telephone.

The Congressman sat there for a long moment. Something was wrong, but even an F.B.I. expert could not see anything. Why would a Chinese guy hold a copy of this book at a vital meeting while typing on his laptop?

In less than forty-eight hours, I will be in Florida, which may be the first question I will ask one of the detainees.

CHAPTER TWENTY

Outside of the Box

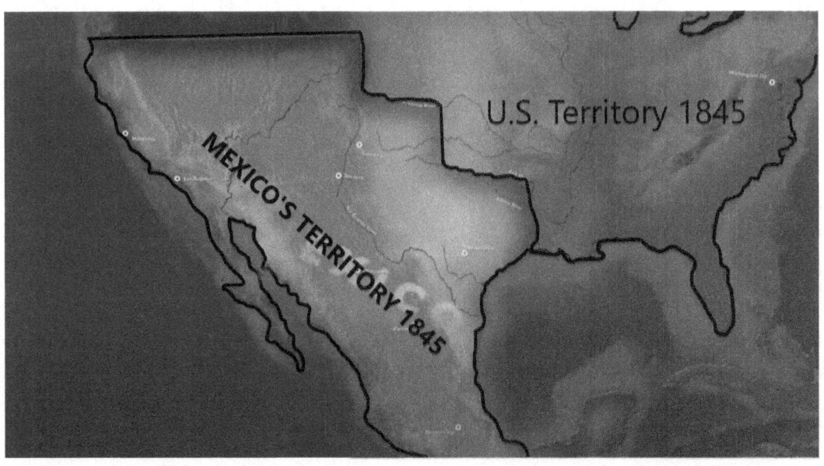

Eleven a.m. in the morning is when Congressman Harris found himself standing at the main entrance of the new Black Ice detention Center in Florida. An early flight and short car ride placed him right where he hoped to find the answers to his many questions. The large glass door swung open, and he stepped into facility security, guarding all entry and exit points.

He reached into his pocket for his identification, and the security agent stopped him, saying, "No need for that, Sir. We know who you are, and we were expecting you. Agent Wilhelm will be down shortly and take you to the interview room." The Congressman stood momentarily and asked where he could find a restroom. The Agent pointed down the hall without saying a word. The Congressman strolled down the hall, checking the signs. Ah, 'Ladies,' 'Gentlemen,' and he stopped momentarily, wondering if he would see a sign saying 'Others or Not Sure.' The Congressman felt sure he was a man and entered the 'Gentlemen's' room to relieve himself.

Upon returning to the entrance area, he saw another agent whom he believed to be Agent Wilhelm. He extended his hand, saying, "Agent Wilhelm, I believe?" A smile and nod echoed the affirmative, and the two men shook hands and started down the hallway leading to the interview room. The main facility turned from a well-windowed area into a block-lined walking area with no windows. A key opened a heavy steel door and allowed the men to enter the secure area of the detention center. The only light in the hallway was the single row of fluorescent lights mounted in dropped ceiling panels, and the reflection of the light from the polished cement floor gave notice of a secure prison environment. A single door led to the interview room as they arrived near the end of the hallway. Passing through the door, Agent Wilhelm spoke for the first time. "Sir, this room is equipped with video and audio recording equipment. Two cameras and three microphones. The Detainee will be cuffed and chained to the table for safety, as we do not know who these people are or what they are capable of. For all we know, they may hold a 'black belt' in martial arts, and we must always keep you and my staff safe." The Congressman nods his head in approval. Congressman Harris asks, "I think I want to start with one of the guys that had the book, 'We Are the Dragons' first, If I may." Agent Wilhelm replies, "I thought you might want to start with them, so they are both nearby."

Agent Wilhelm left the room briefly and returned with another agent and the Detainee. The Detainee was taken over and chained to the metal table, and the Agent moved away to the only entry door.

The Congressman said, "I believe you speak and understand English. Is that correct?" The Detainee nodded his head in agreement. The Congressman continued, "Do you speak or write in any other language?" The Detainee looked at the Congressman and said, "Chinese, read and write." The Congressman moved on, "That's great. Maybe we can get you a job in the State Department as a translator or something." The Detainee sat expressionless at the comment.

The Congressman changed his line of questioning with, "Why did you come to the United States, and by what way did you get here? The Detainee looked directly at Congressman Harris and replied, "I flew my ass here looking for a better life. Does that answer your stupid question?" The Congressman took his chance and said, "We know about the book and what it contains." The Detainee looks at the floor and says, "I don't know what book you are talking about." The Congressman could sense he had struck a cord and continued, "You know, 'We Are the Dragons,' and paused momentarily. We are rounding you guys up to display on the evening news for Chinese officials who watch our news. I am not sure yet which one of you guys we will say told us about the book, but we are working on that." The Detainee sat defiant, but the Congressman saw he was going down the right path for information. The Congressman sat back in his chair, remembering what Professor Norris told him, 'They were proud people and would rather die than lose face or respect.' Looking at the ceiling, the Congressman says, "Of Course, I am sure China will work to get their hackers back out of the U.S. to protect them from our legal system so they won't face the death penalty, but then too, maybe not as the hackers are expendable."

The Detainee started to sweat even though the room was very cool. The Congressman could also see the Detainee would not talk about the book. The Congressman stood and directed the Agent at the door to return the Detainee to his holding cell. As the Detainee left the room, he felt the book was the key to the hackers' plan. Harris also felt sure that the hackers would not talk about what was in the book until the Congressman could disclose a small part of it during an interview. He knew he needed to be able to point to a page in the book and state this is what it says right here and how you will do it. But as of today, that was out of his reach, and further interviews would prove fruitless.

Congressman Harris turned to Agent Wilhem before speaking, "I need the two books you have taken from the Detainees, and I need a flight back to Washington today. Can you make those two things happen?" Agent Wilhelm replies, "Sir, I will have the two books in your hands in ten minutes and your ass on a flight in one hour back to Washington. It may be in a military aircraft, but I will see what I can do. Will that be okay, Sir?" The Congressman looked at the Agent, "I will fly coach if needed."

After eight p.m., the Congressman arrived at his home in Washington. His only thoughts after the flight were that he would never offer to fly coach again. With a briefcase loaded with documents and two hardcover kid's books, Harris dropped them into a chair. It was still early, but after traveling all day, he called it a night and climbed the stairs to bed.

The following day, the Congressman sat at his desk, thumbing through two hardcover books of 'We Are the Dragons.' He could see no notes or markings made by the Detainees anywhere in the books. He knew he held the answer but was like a child looking at bright pictures of mythical creatures. It was almost ten in the morning when he pressed the intercom button, "Bill, could you come in here, please." A minute later, Bill, his secretary, sat in a chair before the Congressman's large desk.

The Congressman sat with his hands folded together and started to speak, "Bill, I have a problem. I have these two books on my desk, and I believe American lives may depend on my understanding of what they mean and to whom." Bill picks up one of the books and opens it. "Well, Sir," Bill says, "They look like a child's book to me. Why do you think they are important?" Congressman Harris sits forward before speaking, "What I am about to tell you, Bill, must be in the strictest confidence. Agents took these two books from people we believed were Chinese hackers. I can't prove that because I don't know what these books are about. I had the F.B.I. look at them, but the best thing the F.B.I. got was that they were poorly written kids' books. I don't believe that for a minute. When I mentioned these books, I witnessed a Chinese detainee break into a sweat in a cool room. There is something in them, and I do not know where to turn for help. Any ideas of someone, I don't care who, someone who can help figure these damn books out?"

Bill sat looking around the room and then said, "Sometimes, Sir, you need to think outside of the box. You need to get someone who does not follow the rules, so to speak. I knew one guy from upstate New York who could figure out anything. Maybe someone like him would take a look at them for you. I warn you, Sir, he is one of those computer guys that will scare you, but if anyone can figure it out, he could." The Congressman looks at Bill, "Please tell me he is not one of the crackpots with a computer." Bill replies, "Sir, from what I am looking at in your face, I would settle for a crackpot if he can figure it out." As Bill stood to leave the room, the Congressman said, "How do we get a hold of the crackpot." Bill replies, "That's easy. I look under the word trouble, and I can find him." The Congressman says, "His name is really trouble?" Bill looks back, "No, but close enough, I will get him here."

Two days later, the crackpot arrived at the Congressman's office in Washington, D.C., at the request of the Congressman's secretary. Not knowing what to expect, the Congressman exited his private office and approached the man cautiously. Extending his hand, he introduces himself, "Hello, I am Congressman Harris, and your name is?" The stranger responds, "Ken, just, Ken." "Well, good to meet you, Ken. I hope you can help me with a little problem." Ken lays down the case he was carrying on the floor before responding, "First of all, you did not pay my way down to Washington for a little problem. I do not want to spend much time in D.C., which is far too dangerous here. Bill said something about some books, so instead of wasting a lot of time filibustering, where are the books so I can get started?" The Congressman went into his office and returned carrying the two books. The Congressman asks, "Now be careful with these books. They cost over forty-two dollars each. Do you speak Chinese?" Ken replies, "Sir, I barely speak English, which I have found to be an advantage when dealing with problems. Now, where can I set up to work?" Bill pointed to a small spare office off the main area, and Ken entered and began to set up shop.

Ken removed a larger-than-normal laptop from his case, placed it on the small desk, and plugged it in. "Where did you get that laptop?" Bill asked. "I built it out of spare parts for special applications," Ken responded. Ken lifted the two books and asked, "Are these the only copies of the book?" Congressman Harris responds, "The only other copy is an electronic download I got from Amazon." Ken dipped into his pocket and handed the Congressman a thumb drive, "Here, copy the book's electronic version onto this and give it back to me."

The Congressman returned to his office, copied the book's electronic version onto the thumb drive, returned to the small office, and handed it to Ken. Bill asks, "Is there anything else you will need?" Ken replies, "A six-pack of Pepsi and some potato chips, the barbeque kind." And closes the door to the small office.

The Congressman signals Bill to follow him into his office and says, "Close the door, please. Outside the box, this guy doesn't even live in the same universe we live in. Maybe he could use something else like a new car or house." Bill replies, "He did mention a car would be nice." The Congressman shaking his head, "If that guy can tell me what is in those books, I will buy him a damn car. The F.B.I. went over the book and found nothing, and now we have Ken the wiz kid in there trying to save the country. Bill, I have things to do. Let me know if he figures out anything." Bill turned and left the room, closing the door behind him.

The clock on the wall showed two hours had passed before any discernable motion in the small office. The small office door opened, and Ken emerged holding one of the books, mumbling that someone was an idiot. Ken looks at Bill before speaking. "Could you please have the Congressman come in here?"

As the Congressman enters the small office, Ken asks, "Why didn't you tell me the electronic download was only three dollars? I needed to go to Amazon to find that out." The Congressman asks, "What does the difference in cost mean?" Ken replies, "They don't want you to buy the hardcovered book, so they over-priced it so you would only buy the electronic version." The Congressman looks to Bill before asking, "Why does that matter anyway?" Ken shakes his head before replying, "Because the books are different, that's why!"

Ken moves to the single desk and says, "Look at my computer screen. I scanned the first page of the hardcover book because I noticed that the Chinese characters did not look the same as the electronic version. Here is what I found in the middle of a sentence not in the electronic version:

巴尔的摩大桥

The Congressman and Bill stared at the screen before saying together, "So." Ken replies, "That says Baltimore Bridge in Chinese. The next sentence informed the reader to use the picture on page fifteen of the electronic version. Here is what I found when I did that using the parsing software I developed." The Congressman and Bill watched Ken change the computer screen to monitoring software.

Ken starts, "This code is encrypted into the pictures of the electronic version of 'We Are the Dragons' book. It is a hacker's code that gets into systems that control things around the United States. Here is what the code looks like to the hacker when he strips it out of the picture. Ken presses a few keys and displays the following hacker computer code:"

```
Okay: import os\nimport sys\n\nimport six\n\nimport hacking
    Okay: import six\nimport znon_existent_package
    Okay: import os\nimport threading
    S366: import mock\nimport os
    S366: import hacking\nimport os
    S366: import hacking\nimport nonexistent
    S366: import hacking\nimport mock
    """
    if (noqa or blank_before > 0 or
            indent_level != previous_indent_level):
        return

normalized_line = core.import_normalize(logical_line.strip()).split()
    normalized_previous = core.import_normalize(previous_logical.
                                        strip()).split()

    def compatible(previous, current):
        if previous == current:
            return True

    if normalized_line and normalized_line[0] == 'import':
        current_type = _get_import_type(normalized_line[1])
        if normalized_previous and normalized_previous[0] == 'import':
            previous_type = _get_import_type(normalized_previous[1])
            if not compatible(previous_type, current_type):
                yield(0, 'S366: imports not grouped correctly '
                    '(%s: %s, %s: %s)' %
                    (normalized_previous[1], previous_type,
                     normalized_line[1], current_type))
version_list = version.split('.')
    version_list[-1] = str(int(version_list[-1]) - 1)
    previous_version = '.'.join(version_list)

    content = template.render(ver=version, prev_ver=previous_version)
    return content

def write_guide(version, guide_content):
    filename = 'porting_guide_{0}.rst'.format(version)
    with open(filename, 'w') as out_file:
        out_file.write(guide_content)

class PortingGuideCommand(Command):
    name = 'porting-guide'

    @classmethod
    def init_parser(cls, add_parser):
```

Ken continues, "This is likely the code that took down the Baltimore Bridge a while back. I am not done yet. Here is more of the hardcover book:

金门大桥

This references the Golden Gate Bridge, and the picture containing the hacker's code is on another page in the electronic download book telling a hacker how to attack it.

切萨皮克湾大桥

This references the Chesapeake Bay Bridge, and the picture containing the hacker's code is on yet another page of the electronic download book on how to attack it. These structures are all through the hardcovers. Most, even Chinese, would miss the inserted words, but my computer tried to make sense of it and failed. It presented it to me as an error in the book's writing.

The hackers needed both books and, so no one would purchase the hardcover; they priced it very high. Only the hackers would buy the expensive book because they needed it to go with the electronic version. They need both the electronic and printed versions to make things work. Congressman, do you know how many hardcover books were purchased?"

The Congressman stepped back before answering, "Twenty-four hardcover and twenty-four electronic versions." Ken lowers his head before speaking, "Well, that's the number of Chinese hackers you are looking for, twenty-four." The Congressman looks at Ken and says, "How do you know they will all be Chinese." Ken looks at the Congressman before speaking, "Who the hell else do you know that can read that book? And there is one more thing you must consider. For the hacker to execute code of this type, they need a place where they will not be disturbed, and it would require a lot of bandwidth on the Internet. An apartment would not be suitable for such a task." Congressman Harris paused and replied, "We know the Mexican Cartels have been setting up control centers across the U.S. because we found a few of them. Would they do?" Ken says, "That would be a perfect place, quiet and without a doubt large bandwidth to the Internet, but there is the question of how the hackers would be able to find the control centers. You know, in the back part of the electronic version of the book, there are eight more pictures than in the hardcover. Those pictures were under the title of places where Dragons live. I think that is where the addresses of the Cartel control centers are stored. The electronic version could be updated weekly on Amazon with additional or new addresses. Congressman, have the F.B.I. scan those images with Criptor Seven version nine and see if the Cartel control centers addresses are in those images." The Congressman looks toward Bill before speaking, "How do you know about a program the F.B.I. has to scan images for encrypted data?" As Ken continues to pick up his computer things, he answers without looking up, "Because I wrote it for them, that's how!"

The Congressman thanks Ken before he leaves the small office. He walks into his private office and signals Bill to join him while Ken packs up his things.

Congressman Harris starts, "I knew I had found the right guy as soon as he walked into the office. Bill, see what kind of car Ken wants, and I will find it somewhere within my budget." Bill turned and left the Congressman's office, shaking his head without saying a word. Bill stopped and called into the small office to inform Ken they were going shopping. Ken asks, "What are we going shopping for?" Bill smiles, looks at Ken, and replies, "Wonderful things, Ken, wonderful things."

The Congressman sat at his desk, and he heard the front door of the office close as Bill and Ken left. Congressman Harris leaned back and closed his eyes, thinking, 'Now you son of a bitches, I can tell you what is in your damn book."

CHAPTER TWENTY-ONE
Satisfaction

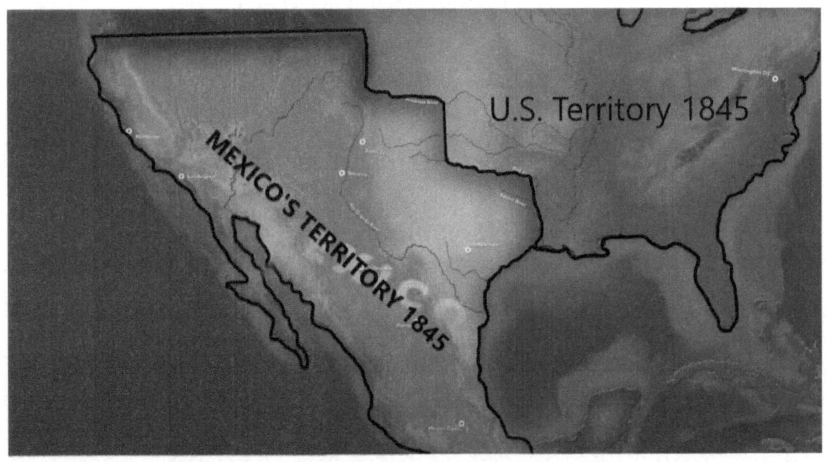

There are few things more satisfying than figuring out a puzzle. That's the Aha moment when everything comes together and makes sense. Solving a puzzle gives you that priceless moment when you feel true satisfaction with yourself. As Congressman Harris sat in his comfortable office chair, he enjoyed one of the special moments.

Unfortunately, solving the puzzle was not the end of the road. It was the beginning of a long list of things that the Congressman needed to do and do now. Leaning forward to access his computer, he opens the contacts list in his e-mail. Scrolling down the long list of contacts, the Congressman located the one sought: the United States Attorney's Office. Lifting the telephone, he dials and waits for an answer. "Hello, this is the United States Attorney's Office with whom am I speaking." Said a soft voice on the other end of the phone. The Congressman replies, "This is Congressman Harris. I need to speak with the U.S. Attorney, and yes, I must speak with him immediately."

The soft voice replies, "I believe he is in his office, Congressman. Please hold for a moment." The telephone was now filled with music that only deaf people would want to hear. The Congressman was in the middle of a thought that maybe he should introduce legislation for funds for better on-hold music when the U.S. Attorney picked up the phone. "Hello, Congressman, what seems to be the emergency?" Asked the U.S. Attorney. The Congressman responds, "Sir, I need you in my office as soon as possible. Lives may depend on how fast we can act. What I have in my office will tell you all you need to know to proceed. When can I expect you?" The voice on the other end of the phone says, "My office is not far from you. I will be there in twenty minutes. Can you give me a clue as to what you have in your office, Sir?" The Congressman's one-word reply, "Dragons," ended the conversation. The telephone disconnected, and the Congressman again sat back in his chair to await the U.S. Attorney's arrival.

Twenty-five minutes later, the U.S. Attorney, William Bart, opened the Congressman's front door. The Congressman greeted him with a firm handshake and a smile. Bart started the conversation, "I am not familiar with the code name of Dragons. Sir, can you bring me up to speed?" The Congressman leads Mr. Bart into his private office and pulls up the book 'We Are the Dragons' on the computer screen. Bart stares at the bright-colored Dragon on the screen and asks, "What am I looking at or for?" This book is part of the hackers handbook used to take down the Baltimore Bridge a while ago. There is a sister book in hardcover that contains the references to the target, and this book, in the images, has the hacker code embedded to accomplish the mission. Mr. Bart looks up at the Congressman before speaking, "And you can prove these books contain this code within them?" The Congressman replies, "I hired one of the best computer people in the country to decode the two books. I found this person because he had previously written special programs for the F.B.I. and knew of his unique qualifications. Here are the reports he printed out within the last two hours with the details of the code used to take down the Baltimore Bridge."

U.S. Attorney Bart studied the printouts carefully before speaking, "From what I am reading here, these hackers have a list of U.S. targets." The Congressman interrupts, "These books, as far as I know, are only available on Amazon. I recommend a 'Cease and Desist' order from a Federal Judge to stop selling or distributing these books served on Amazon. That action will stop additional hackers from gaining access to the books. My computer person also informed me that in the back of the electronic version of the book, there are eight additional images not found within the hardcover. My next call is to the F.B.I. Washington Office to have them scan those images with Criptor Seven version nine to recover the addresses of Cartel control centers around the United States." Mr. Bart walked back and forth across the room for a few seconds before speaking, "Congressman, I will need these copies of the report pages and a copy of the front of the hardcover book. Based on what you have presented here, I should have a Federal Judge issuance of the 'Cease and Desist' order within an hour. I will speak with the attorneys at Amazon and serve them electronically today. That should remove the books immediately from their site. And Sir, I think you are correct. Let's call this operation code name Dragons. Please advise me what the F.B.I. can figure out as soon as you call. You will need to excuse me, Sir. I have work to do to get this order served.

Goodbye." The U.S. Attorney picked up the needed copies of materials and left the office.

The Congressman took a needed restroom break before picking up the phone. Again dialing the F.B.I. Washington Office, he waited for the phone to answer. As soon as the telephone picked up, the Congressman said, "This is Congressman Harris. I need to speak with Agent Zhōu." Without hesitation or questions, the voice on the other end of the line replied, "Yes, Sir," and placed the telephone on hold. When the phone picked up, Agent Zhōu was on the line, "What can I do for you today, Sir." The Congressman replies, "The book 'We Are the Dragons,' I want you to scan the last eight images with Criptor Seven version nine to see if the images contain addresses of places around the United States." The phone went silent momentarily, "Sir, how did you find out about Criptor Seven?" The Congressman says very slowly, "Agent Zhōu, how Congress finds things out is not at issue here. Please scan the images and let me know today if they contain addresses. I suspect they do. Thank you, and please get this done today." And the Congressman hung up the phone.

Looking out through the private office door, he could see the clock on the outer office wall displayed four-thirty, and the Congressman was still waiting for his secretary, Bill, to return from the special shopping trip he and Ken went on. In his mind, the Congressman tried to come up with another word for a car to include on his expense account. Let's look at words like service vehicles, transport vehicles, test vehicles, and security vehicles. Damn, no matter what, the wording always ended in vehicle. I'll need to wait for Bill to return, and maybe he can devise a better word for a car on the expense account.

It was five minutes to five when Bill opened the office's front door. The Congressman's first words were, "Okay, how much was the car?" Bill replied, "Sir, Ken picked out a Hyundai small S.U.V. for under thirty thousand. Wanted something good on gas." The Congressman returned to his desk, thinking he was right. The guy was a crackpot. Anyone else would have picked out a Mercedes or Lincoln. Whatever he picked out made little difference, as Ken may have saved countless lives in two hours.

The Congressman's thoughts were interrupted by the ringing of the office telephone. Bill answered the phone, and the Congressman could hear him say I will get him for you. Bill's voice relays the message, "Agent Zhōu from the F.B.I. Sir, on the secure line."

The Congressman picks up the telephone and asks, "What do you have? Any addresses hidden in the images?" Agent Zhōu responded, "I don't know how you guessed that Sir, but there appears to be a list of addresses from almost every state embedded within the images. I am unsure what the addresses relate to, but they are valid, as I checked a few. And, Sir, one last thing. How did you know about Criptor Seven?" The Congressman replied, "The K.G.B. contacted me about it. I will advise you tomorrow about what we will do with the address information. Goodbye Agent Zhōu." And the Congressman hung up the telephone.

Bill had overheard the part concerning the K.G.B. while the Congressman was on the phone with the F.B.I. Agent. Looking into the Congressman's private office, Bill asks, "Did the K.G.B. tell you about something, Sir?" The Congressman shook his head and replied, "Bill, it is getting late. Please go home and get a good night's rest, as we have a busy day tomorrow." Bill turned, picked up his things, and exited the front office door.

A few minutes later, the Congressman followed through the front door and headed home for a much-needed rest.

The Dragon Slayer

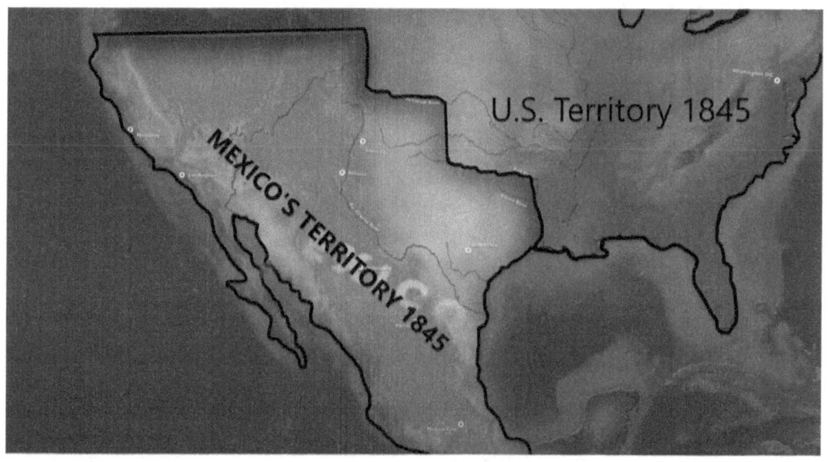

At nine a.m. the following morning, Congressman Harris was on the telephone with the Federal Bureau of Investigation Director, Christopher Ryan. Agent Zhōu had already informed Director Ryan about finding valid addresses hidden in images in a Chinese book. Congressman Harris fills in the missing parts for the Director, "Sir, an informant brought to my attention the existence of this book or books. Agent Zhōu attempted to evaluate one of them by reading the text but to no avail. I had a specialist come into my office and scan them with special software, and that is when we discovered the hidden information. My specialist found apparent reference to the Baltimore Bridge and the hacking code used to take it down." The Director interjects, "Yes, I was contacted last evening by the U.S. Attorney concerning the books. He believes they are authentic and has obtained an injunction against their sale and distribution. Our next step, Congressman, is to place round-the-clock surveillance at each address. It should be interesting to see why someone would hide addresses within images in a kid's book. Especially a Chinese kid's book." The Congressman finishes, "Well, Director, I am leaving the investigation parts to you and your agents. I have some matters to address in Florida later today, and I need to gather some things for the trip." Director Ryan replies, "Have a safe trip, Sir, and if you find out anything or need assistance, my entire agency is at your disposal. Goodbye Congressman." And the telephone disconnected.

Three hours later, the Congressman stood in a boarding line at Reagan International Airport heading to Florida to visit the Black Ice detention center. With him, he had one of the hardcover books and his laptop with the electronic version, in another folder in his briefcase, copies of the decoded book pages that disclosed the true meaning of the books. Today's interviews will be directed at the detainees who possessed copies of the books, as they would be the hackers they sought.

The two-and-a-half-hour flight was uneventful, with nothing falling off of the aircraft. The Congressman's flight was even more pleasant as he flew first class and had something to eat. Landing at the Florida Airport in Tampa, the Black Ice Agent was waiting to take him to the detention facility about a half hour away. In a short time, Congressman Harris stood at the main entrance of the new Black Ice detention Center in Florida. The large glass door opened, and he stepped inside to be greeted by Agent Wilhelm in the center's central area.

"Do you need to use the restroom, Sir?" Said Wilhelm. The Congressman replies, "No, I relieved myself at the airport when I landed. I want to get this interview over and head back to D.C."

"This way, Sir, I have the person you want to speak with already in the room," and they traveled down the hallway to the interview room. As they opened the door and stepped in, their favorite Detainee, who claimed to know nothing, was already seated and chained with the single Agent inside the door.

The Congressman sat in his chair before saying, "Good afternoon, Sir. I hope you are doing well. Are you being treated fairly here?" There was a pause for an answer, but no answer was forthcoming. "Well, I'll take that as a yes." Said the Congressman. He continued, "The last time I was here, we talked about a book." The Detainee chirps, "I never said anything about a book." "Oh, that's right, I was talking about a book." Said the Congressman. "Then let me continue with what I was talking about." The Congressman continued. "But before I do, can you please tell me if you have relatives living in the United States or Mexico waiting to come to the United States?" The Detainee looks up, "Yeah, my mother, father, and little sister live in the United States. Why? Are you going to arrest them?" The Congressman replies, "Absolutely not. I asked you so I could protect them from the people you 'ratted out' when you told the Federal Agents about the books. "The Detainee's head moved quickly back and forth before speaking, "I never told anybody anything, and you know it. Do you think I am stupid enough to say anything?"

The Congressman digs into his briefcase before replying, "Well, maybe someone else did the ratting. Let me check something. No, it says right here that you are the one who told the Agents what was in the books." The Detainee tried to stand while yelling, "That's a lie, and you know it." Congressman Harris slides a document from a folder on the table before speaking, "Sir, look right here is what you told the Agents. This Chinese set of symbols means Baltimore Bridge, and it references the electronic version of the book. It gives this code for hacking the power and communication systems at the bridge that caused the collision. Here, take a good look. I am sure you will remember it. Here, look." The Detainee barks, "I don't know what you are trying to pull, but I am not going along with it. Do you understand me?"

Congressman Harris slides his chair back a little before continuing, "Sir, we have the book we found in your possession and an electronic version of the book on your computer. The last eight images contain the address where you went to take down the bridge. Sir, it is all right here. You killed several workers on the Baltimore Bridge when you hacked into the guidance and support systems. The code is right here, Sir." "You can't prove that." The Detainee screamed. "Prove," Started the Congressman, "I don't intend to prove anything. I intend to go before the Cameras tomorrow and announce that you are the hacker who caused the Bridge collision. I will also lay out how you explained how the books work and how the Chinese government trained and sent twenty-four of you hackers to disrupt the United States. I will make a special point of informing everyone how we could not have broken the case without your help."

The Detainee sat straight up before speaking, "You are going to get my family killed." Congressman Harris takes a moment before replying, "No, Sir, you are going to get your entire family killed, not us, you. Someone told me the Chinese are a proud race of people who will do anything not to soil the name and image of their family.

You, Sir, will be remembered as the person and family who betrayed China for eternity. We have a person like that in American history. His name is Benedict Arnold. Maybe you have heard of him?"

The Congressman pauses again before speaking, "I know you have the identity of the other hackers sent by China. I want the names. I would like to know where you trained and how you arrived. I want to know how high in the Chinese government this hacker project reaches. If you give me that information, I will have no reason to announce anything to anyone. Your family and family name will be safe. After all, I already have all the information about your team's planning, so you are giving us nothing we do not have. My plan is simple: as we round up your hacker team, Agents will bring them here for an interview. As a bonus, anyone who cooperates with us, the United States government will protect their families from the Chinese and the Cartels. I have just presented here, Sir, the deal I intend to offer each hacker to end this nightmare for the United States. It will also spare you and your family name. I will need your answer when I return from the men's room."

The Congressman stood and walked through the door and into the hall toward the men's room. The Chinese hacker sat without saying anything, thinking about the offer.

The Congressman returned and said, "Well, Sir, is it a yes or no?" The Detainee nodded his head, agreeing to the Congressman's proposal.

Congressman Harris returned his papers to his briefcase, turned, and left the room. As the Congressman and Agent Wilhelm walked down the hall, Wilhelm asked, "Sir, If you already have the books and know what they say, why would you offer these hackers a deal?" The Congressman stops for a moment, "Well, Wilhelm, I don't want to get their family members killed. But I cannot afford to have any loose ends either. Right now, there are a lot of loose ends I need to tie up."

Wilhelm replies, "I think I understand, Sir. And, by the way, we have picked up another twenty Chinese on the list, and three of them have copies of the book." "Those are the hackers, Wilhelm. Keep them separate until I can interview each of them. But right now, I am needed in Washington." Agent Wilhelm replies, "I understand, Sir. Your transportation will be waiting at the door as you leave the facility. Have a safe trip, Sir." The Congressman stops and says, "Please don't tell me I am flying coach."

Wilhelm waves his hand, saying, "Not this trip, Congressman. Enjoy the flight." Wilhelm turned and walked away.

CHAPTER TWENTY-THREE
No Stone Left Unturned

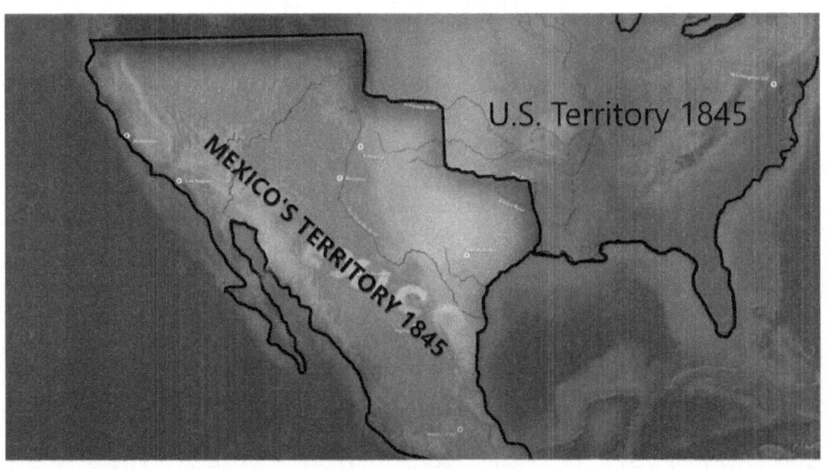

Friday morning just after sunrise in Elmira, New York, a small town in the Upstate region that is the home of Professor Norris. A loud knock on the door of the Professor's home awakens all within. A voice follows the knock, informing the residents that the F.B.I. has a search warrant to search the house. The Professor wanders to the front door with his wife trailing close behind. As he opened the door, the Professor and his wife were confronted by several men dressed in full battle gear, proudly displaying the large letters F.B.I. and demanding access to the home.

The Agent in the doorway addresses the couple, "Please step back. We have a warrant to search this resident and seize any electronics, telephones, documents, or other written materials pertinent to our investigation. Do you have any weapons in the home?" The Professor replies, "Well, I believe my son has an old B.B. gun in a bedroom closet upstairs, but I don't know if it works. Please take it to the yard area to test it."

The Agents pushed past the couple as they stood barefoot in their robes. The Agent asks, "Is your son at home?" The Professor's wife answers, "No, I think he is over at the Watson's house or maybe the Jenkin's place. Should I call for him? He is eleven, but I don't believe he has broken any Federal laws."

Professor Norris attempts to address the elephant in the room by saying, "Why are you here raiding my home, and what are you searching for?" The lead Agent hands the Professor the search warrant before saying, "I will ask the questions here today. Please move into the living room so I can speak with you." After walking and sitting in the living room, the lead Agent begins the interrogation with, "Anything you say here today can and will be used against you in a court of law. Do you understand that?" The Professor answers, "Of course, we understand that.

Don't you think we watch the movies?" The Professor's wife speaks, "Can I get you gentlemen anything? I have coffee and tea. And I may also have some light beer in the refrigerator."

The Agent continues, "Have you or your wife contacted any foreign government over the last eighteen months for any reason? The Professor took a moment to think about the question for a minute before speaking, "I have spoken with an official of the Egyptian government a while back." The Agent leans forward to ask, "And what was that interaction about?" The Professor replies, "Tickets, yes tickets, they wanted tickets to my New York City seminar on the history of the Middle East and how it affects the world economy. Oh my, I took the mailing cost as a tax deduction for mailing the tickets. Is that why you are here?" The Agent sits back and continues, "Have you spoken with any Chinese people recently?" The Professor turns his head and replies, "Yes." The Agent again leans forward and says, "And who were the Chinese people you spoke with?" The Professor answers, "The couple across the street. They moved here just over a year ago and are the nicest people you could ever meet."

One of the two Agents searching the area adjacent to the living room overheard the conversation and remarked to the other, "Coolest two people I have ever witnessed under pressure; what do you think?" Agent Louis replies, "Those two are a highly trained and disciplined pair up to something nefarious ."

The lead Agent sat back and took a break as the other agents searched the home, securing computers, telephones, and any papers they thought were relevant. The home search continued for over an hour when one of the agents approached the Lead Agent in the living room. Standing in the doorway, the Agent spoke, "I think we have everything, Sir. Should I take the B.B. gun with us?" The lead Agent stood and replied, "No, leave the B.B. gun here." The Professor asks, "Sir, when can we get our things back?" The lead Agent replies, "We will send them to Washington to determine what you have been up to. After that, the government may or may not return the items."

The Agents placed the Professor's family's belongings into protective evidence bags and left the home. The Professor and his wife sat on the living room couch, looking at each other. The Professor leaned over, kissed his wife on her forehead, and said, "I think we have just witnessed the Federal Government in its finest moments."

Congressman Harris was seated in his office when the call came in from the U.S. Attorney. The U.S. Attorney started the conversation slowly, "Congressman, hey listen, for some reason unknown to me, the Northern District of New York Attorney had a search warrant issued against Professor Norris and his family. The F.B.I. raided his home before seven this morning. Are you still there?" "Yes, I am here." Said the Congressman. The Congressman continues, "And why, may I ask, would the Northern District of New York Attorney do that?" The U.S. Attorney responds, "From what I can gather, the Northern District Attorney felt the Professor knew too much about what was going on, so he got a judge to sign a warrant to search the home." The Congressman asks, "Did it ever occur to the Northern District Attorney that a Professor of History would know about countries and their history? The U.S. Attorney replies, "I don't know and cannot answer that Sir." The Congressman replies, "I want that Attorney's direct telephone number right now. I also want you to call him and inform him he will receive a call from me in ten minutes. I expect him to answer the telephone when I call personally. After you call that Attorney, I would like you to personally locate the Professor's belongings and make sure they stay at that location. Have I made myself clear here today, Sir?" The U.S. Attorney replies, "Clear, and I will get those things done right now." And the telephone hung up.

The Congressman stood and shook his head in a gesture of total disbelief. He walked back and forth in his office thinking, why would the Northern District Attorney take it upon himself to have a warrant issued to search a Professor's home? The Congressman picked up the phone and dialed the direct number of the Northern District Attorney's Office. "Hello, is this Congressman Harris?" Said the voice that answered the phone. Trying to maintain his composure, the Congressman replies, "Yes, this is Congressman Harris. Please do not say a word and listen to what I am about to say. I don't know how you found out about Professor Norris, and I don't care how you found out. I don't care how you do it, but I want you to locate the Professor's property and return it personally. You tell the Professor the whole thing was some mistake, and the government wants to make the inconvenience up to him and his family. You will give him your personal credit card information and book a reservation at the Torra Bar & Restaurant in Manhattan for him and his family; I know he likes it there, and also pay for the transportation." The phone remained silent, and Congressman Harris continued, "You will also pay for any damages to the Professor's property. Let them in-spect it when you return it today." The Attorney responds, "Today, Sir, today is my anniversary, and I have a dinner date with my wife." The Congressman interrupts, "No, Mr. Northern District of New York Attorney, tonight you have a date returning Professor Norris's property and making arrangements for them in New York City. If, for some reason, you can not make this happen, you will have plenty of time starting tomorrow to spend with your wife looking for a job. Remember, you work at the pleasure of the President, and Sir, if you can not get this done tonight, he will show his displeasure with you tomorrow morning by firing you. I need Professor Norris's help a lot more than I need you. Any questions?" The response was, "I will get it done tonight." The Congressman finishes, "I will call the Professor, voice my apologies for what happened, and inform him that you will address this problem tonight. If I do not get a call from the Professor this evening indicating you made everything right, consider yourself an ex-attorney in the morning. Goodbye." And the Congressman hung up the telephone.

CHAPTER TWENTY-FOUR

The Wait

The Fiasco caused by the Northern District of New York Attorney a few days prior was finally settling down. As directed, the Attorney recovered and returned the Professor's belongings later that day. That evening, on the telephone, the Professor thanked the Congressman and commented that he and his wife were the neighborhood celebrities for being raided by the F.B.I. Everyone wanted to hear the story about the shakedown by the Feds and how exciting it must have been. The Congressman's only reply was he was glad he could help out and bring some excitement to their lives.

But for now, the Congressman was in wait mode. It had been three long weeks since Congressman Harris's last visit to the Black Ice detention center in Florida for Chinese hacker interviews. Three weeks that seemed like an eternity to the Congressman. To date, the Congressman had interviewed twenty-three known hackers, and after hearing the deal, the Congressman put forth, each agreed to the terms of no public humiliation of their families. Professor Norris was correct when he stated that Chinese honor was more valuable than their lives.

The Congressman sat by and waited patiently for the telephone to ring and to hear Agent Wilhelm proclaim the magic words, "We got number twenty-four, the last one!" Until that time, all other agencies were placed in standby mode, waiting to spring the trap and shut down the Cartel control centers around the United States.

The Director of the F.B.I. had made numerous appearances before Congressional Committees, sounding the warnings of possible attacks by the many unknowns that invaded the country by way of the Southern border. All his appearances were televised by cable T.V. across the country, placing the entire country on edge. Like throwing gasoline on a fire, the citizens of the United States began seeing specters of terrorists in every corner, some real and some not, but all a threat to their imagination.

Yesterday, an attack on the Golden Gate Bridge, launched by the last of the at-large Chinese hackers, failed because of the excellent work done by Ken, A.K.A. the Crackpot. Ken had accessed the hacker code hidden in the book 'We Are the Dragons' and programmed new firewalls into the Bridge's secured system, blocking access to the hacker.

The reports for The Republic of Sanctuary trickled in and showed a steady growth in the population of the Republic, now numbering over three thousand residents. Another body had been recovered and laid to rest in the cemetery on the southern end of the Republic. And true to form the body was that of a prominent gang leader known for his cruelty.

The Black Ice agents stationed across the country were doing their job and working with every state and city to remove these undesirables from the United States. The once-sanctuary cities nationwide were only sanctuaries if the undocumented followed the law. Failing to do so exposed you to the long arm of the Black Ice group and likely disappeared to a mythical place, a world with no escape. By any measure, The Republic of Sancturay was a significant success and was reducing undocumented violent crime across the United States.

It was late afternoon when Bill, the Congressman's secretary, informed him Agent Wilhelm was on the phone. The Congressman slowly picked up the telephone and said, "Hello." Agent Wilhelm responded, "We got number twenty-four here at the detention center." The Congressman leans back and responds, "Great job, Wilhelm, we finally got them all. This one belongs to you, Wilhelm; you watched me make a deal with the first twenty-three; you present the deal and finish the last one. He is all yours, Wilhelm. I have things to do here in Washington. Thank you, see you soon." The Congressman hung up the phone.

The Congressman lifted the telephone and dialed the U.S. Attorney in Washington, D.C. Christopher Ryan, the U.S. Attorney, answered, "This is Ryan." Congressman Harris made the conversation short and sweet, "Number twenty-four is in the can. I will meet you in the morning to put this to bed." And Hung up the phone.

The long wait was over, and all the Chinese hackers were now in custody in the Black Ice Detention Center in Florida. The time had come for the approximately two hundred Homeland Security and F.B.I. Agent groups to execute their mission. They were going to attack each of the Cartel control centers simultaneously around the United States. United States Special Forces trained and armed each group and prepared them for urban warfare if necessary. The Cartels were finally going to meet the steadfast resolve of the United States of America, facing some of the best-trained military-style men the United States had to offer.

The only thing left was finding the right time to execute the plan. "Bill, what's on the President's schedule for the next few weeks," The Congressman asked. His secretary took a moment before replying, "Two speaking engagements next week, and then in ten days, he is having a summit with the South American alliance in Mexico. Then..." The Congressman interrupts, "That's what I needed, ten days a summit in Mexico. Perfect, I got what I needed. Thank you."

The Congressman picked up the telephone and called the White House. When the phone answered, the Congressman said, "This is Congressman Harris. I need to speak with the President's chief of staff." After a short pause, a voice replies, "I am sorry he is not in his office. Can I forward a message?" The Congressman replies, "Please tell the Chief of Staff that the Ambassador for China must be invited to attend the Mexico summit scheduled in the next ten days. It will be imperative he be there. If that is a problem, please ask him to advise me immediately. I repeat, the Ambassador to China must be at the Mexico summit in ten days." The telephone disconnected.

Ten days later, the meeting started on schedule with the President of Mexico and most South American representatives seated around a large table. The special guest, the Ambassador to China, was sitting near the head of the table next to the President of Mexico.

A large screen on the wall lighted and displayed the President of the United States sitting in a chair alongside a bed. The President of the United States began speaking. "I am sorry I could not be there today due to illness. In my place, I have sent Congressman Harris and Professor Norris to address this most important meeting. Consider whatever they may say to be coming directly from me, and any agreement they make will be honored by my office. Again, I sincerely apologize for not being there, but I have left you in capable hands." With that, the monitor went dark, and Congressman Harris walked up and stood at the head of the table.

The Congressman begins and speaks slowly to allow the interpreters to translate his message. "It has been alleged that a meeting took place in northern Mexico, and a plan was laid out to take back territory from the United States that was ceded in the Mexican-American War in 1848. I spoke with the President of Mexico briefly, and he guaranteed no such meeting ever took place, and no such plans were ever discussed. My good friend Professor Norris took part in that meeting with the President of Mexico, and we all agreed that this conspiracy theory was ridiculous and without merit."

The Congressman pauses and continues, reading from documents in his hand, "As of early today, the News reports are: This morning, predawn raids were conducted by the F.B.I. and Homeland Security across the United States on approximately two hundred Cartel control centers. There were reports of heavy resistance, but United States Special Agents have taken each control center. There are several dead, which all appear to be of Mexican descent. From these centers, Special Agents have collected large amounts of drugs, military-grade weapons, and computers containing vast amounts of data on the Cartel's operations."

The room of attendees looked from side to side after hearing about the news articles. Everyone in the room was aware the Cartels had the details of the plan to take down the United States. The question remained: did the Special Agents seize that information stored on the Cartel's computers?

The Congressman waits for the attendees to listen again. "I spoke with the President of Mexico before this meeting today, and he has agreed to repatriate many thousands of the undocumented people who crossed the border over the last several years. We discussed the possibility of a new administration in the United States, and he decided it would be a good gesture.

Today, the President of the United States ordered the United States Military to station along the Mexican-U.S.

Border for the first time since the Cession of 1848. The United States President implemented this measure to protect Mexico from Cartel members trying to cross back into Mexico from the U.S. side of the border."

The Congressman looks over to his left before speaking." I want to address my good friends from China who are attending this meeting today. China has alleged that The United States has detained twenty-four Chinese citizens somewhere in the southern part of the country. To be clear, the United States has detained twenty-four hackers who conspired to attack the United States and have committed acts of war against the United States. My good Chinese friends, please raise your hands if you are acknowledging and responsible for these acts of war executed against the United States by these hackers."

Congressman Harris waited for someone in the Chinese delegation to raise their hand before saying, "Have you ever read the book "We Are the Dragons? Others have advised me it contains some beautiful pictures." Each member of the Chinese delegation shook their heads, denying ever reading such a book. As always, the Chinese delegation sat stoned-faced and defiant to the suggestion they sent the hackers to the United States.

The Congressman turns a page of the documents in his hand and continues, "My good friends from South America. The United States has tried for a long time to help your countries prosper and grow. We have sent billions of dollars of foreign aid to each of your countries each year with little or no accounting. As of today, the United States will suspend all foreign assistance until each of you agrees to repatriate your citizens deported from the U.S. The time has come for you to repair your countries and not dump your unwanted into the United States. The United States will work on foreign aid when you agree to repatriate.

There is one other thing I need to address here today. Please look at the photo I placed before each of you before you were seated. I realize no one here today knows this person in the picture, but it is from the Israeli Intelligence files. I am not asking anyone here to hand over information about this person's location, but locating this person would go a long way in rebuilding trust between our nations. A simple note on the back of the photo will be enough, so please leave the picture on the table when you exit this meeting, and I will gather them up.

Congressman Harris closes with, "Before we leave here today, another thing I will debunk is the mythical place called Sanctuary. The United States Government does not know of or acknowledge the existence of this mythical place called Sanctuary, and it exists only in the minds of people writing conspiracy novels and between the covers of their books. I repeat, only in their minds and between the covers."

The meeting was finally over, and everyone left with their discussion version of what was said in the meeting, each slanted to their advantage. The Congressman had shielded the President from an honest and focused discussion of what the United States needed to once again work with these countries.

One week after the meeting, there was breaking News flying over the cable news networks: "The Head of the Revolutionary Guard Terrorist arm and his staff were located today and killed in a drone attack in Syria after a four-year search for this elusive person. It is unclear how he was located and killed. Still, sources close say a photo with his location appeared to a Congressman in a dream, and the information was turned over to Israeli Intelligence."

It was daybreak on San Nicolas Island. A voice broke the morning silence, "The plane will be arriving in about a half-hour from the States." said the on-duty Agent as he lifted and reads the plane's manifest. "This is strange," he says while scanning the list of names on the manifest. "It says only twenty-seven guests are on the plane today, and twenty-four of them are Chinese."

Back in Washington D.C., Congressman Harris walked the stone-covered path to the place where his wife and daughter had both been laid to rest less than a year before. He sat on the corner of his daughter's head marker and relived better times when the family was still with him. He looked down and began to speak softly to the memories of his family as if they were still there and listening. "I'm sorry I have not gotten up here more to see you guys, but, you know, work and all has kept me very busy."

As he spoke, the Congressman drifted off into the nightmare of almost a year ago. He again heard the squeal of tires, blinding headlights, and the impact of the speeding pickup truck as it crashed into the car he and his wife were traveling in. The truck pushed their car, crushing it against a retaining wall, and he remembered the sense of a warm liquid running into his eyes. The bright red flashing lights lit up the night, and his wife sat beside him motionless. The medics on the scene pulled him from the twisted wreck of the family car, and a voice in the night proclaiming the passenger was dead. His thoughts then flashed back to the court proceeding when he learned the person driving the pickup truck had been deported nine times before that fatal night. The Congressman's wife had just become another number on the wall, counting innocent victims of the undocumented running wild in the country. Another number on a wall, definitely, but she was also the Congressman's beloved wife.

He awoke from the nightmare and continued speaking with his daughter, "I tried to rationalize what happened to your mother as a freak thing that could never happen to us again. I tried until the man from Venezuela assaulted and killed you while you were jogging. I failed you by being blind and following party lines to allow the influx of unvetted people. I failed you, not the system; it was me. The good people of the United States opened their hearts and allowed so many to migrate into this country. Maybe that was reckless. I don't know. We offered a chance for those who could conform to our way of living a better life with work and a shot at true happiness. We, as a country, have never been afraid to share our nation's wealth with anyone. For those people, we hold out our hands and welcome them to our land.

But there are others determined, like the person who killed you, to bring the crime and violence from where they fled to our homes. Honey, I did not let your sacrifice go in vain. For you and all the others like you who have suffered at the hands of those who can not conform, I, no we, have given them the place they were searching for. We delivered them to Sanctuary.

Rest in peace, my little girl, rest in peace."

With tears in his eyes, Congressman Harris lowered his head to pray. As a man, he had done all possible as a human being, and now the rest would require a power much more significant than what he possessed. He prayed for peace on the streets of America, he prayed for the illegal immigrants, and he prayed for the day all this madness would finally end.

The End

www.ingramcontent.com/pod-product-compliance
Lightning Source LLC
Chambersburg PA
CBHW032027310726
48972CB00002B/557